SIEGE AT WATTS' STATION

Several young Apaches break out of the San Carlos Indian Reservation in order to meet renegade gunrunners who want to sell them guns in exchange for furs. Lieutenant Asa Harrington is ordered to find them and finds himself at Watts' Stagecoach Station, together with Timmy O'Brien, a young boy whose parents have been killed by the Indians. Harrington finds he must defend the Station not only against the Indians but against the gunrunners as well!

SIEGE AT WATTS' STATION

by
Steven Gray

Dales Large Print Books
Long Preston, North Yorkshire,
England.

British Library Cataloguing in Publication Data.

Gray, Steven
  Siege at Watts' Station.

  A catalogue record for this book is
  available from the British Library

  ISBN 1-85389-819-8 pbk

First published in Great Britain by Robert Hale Ltd., 1997

Copyright © 1997 by Steven Gray

Cover illustration © Faba by arrangement with Norma Editorial S.A.

Published in Large Print 1998 by arrangement with Robert Hale Ltd.

Dales Large Print is an imprint of
Library Magna Books Ltd.
Printed and bound in Great Britain by
T.J. International Ltd., Cornwall, PL28 8RW.

ONE

The Indian attack came at dawn.

It was still dark outside, the morning a pale streak in the eastern sky. Yawning, bleary-eyed, Philip O'Brien shrugged into his clothes ready to fetch water from the creek before tending to the animals.

One minute everything was normal, quiet, the next the air was full of whoops and cries. Several guns were fired, bullets slapping into the wooden walls.

'What's wrong?' Skillet in one hand, Kathleen, Philip's wife, appeared in the kitchen doorway. She looked very scared. 'Philip, what's going on?'

'I don't know.' O'Brien peered out of the nearest window. His face paled. 'Oh my God!' He turned to her. 'It's Indians. Apaches.'

Kathleen gave a little scream of terror, hand going to her mouth. 'It can't be,' she protested. 'They've been on the Reservation for years. They don't go on the attack, not any more.'

'Well they do now,' O'Brien said grimly. 'Make sure the doors and windows are all shut and barred. Go on!'

He pushed by Kathleen going into the kitchen and took down the rifle from where it hung on pegs on the wall. It wasn't even loaded. The bullets were kept in one of the cabinet drawers. With hands that shook, he loaded the rifle and took it over to the window. The situation was hopeless.

Twenty or more young bucks milled about beyond the corral. Some on horseback. Some on foot. All wore warpaint and feathers, and were armed with guns or bows and arrows. They were getting ready to charge again, their excited yips carrying across the still air to the house.

O'Brien had just the one rifle, his Colt handgun and little spare ammunition for either. He'd never shot at anyone before, let alone killed another man, whereas Apaches were trained in warfare from when they were children.

He didn't understand what was happening, or why.

Kathleen was right. The Apaches had been settled on the San Carlos Reservation for a long while now. Conditions there might not be ideal and they might not be happy about their confinement, but being both guarded and the recipients of government hand-outs meant they rarely caused trouble or broke out; except maybe to go hunting or get drunk. They didn't attack lonely settlers.

'Pop.'

O'Brien swung round from the window. Timmy stood in the doorway, wiping sleep from his eyes. Kathleen came up behind her son, putting her arms around him as if she never wanted to let him go. O'Brien looked at her and read in her eyes the kowledge that was also in his: they were going to die.

He fired once from the window just to let the Indians know they weren't completely defenceless and in the forlorn hope that it would persuade them to go away. Then he put one hand on the boy's shoulder. 'Tim, you must get dressed and go and hide in the cellar. You'll be safe there.'

'I want to stay with you and Mom.'

'No!' O'Brien said, his fingers digging into Timmy's arm. 'You must be strong and brave, for us.'

'But...'

'Do as your father says.' Kathleen hugged Timmy again, kissing him on the cheek. 'We'll be all right. We'll see you in a while.'

O'Brien wanted to shout out at the unfairness of it all, wanted to hold his son, protect him. All he could do was send him off to what he hoped would be a safe hiding place. There was no time for anything else.

For the Indians were charging again.

O'Brien had no choice but to turn his back on Timmy to fire out of the window.

'Timmy, go,' Kathleen urged.

Running back into his bedroom, the boy pulled on his clothes, wishing his hands wouldn't tremble so much. Out in the passageway he opened the trapdoor that led down to the cellar where the provisions were stored in the dark and the cool. He could hear his father shooting steadily even when he closed the trapdoor over his head.

Timmy was ten. He'd never experienced Indian warfare before but he'd heard stories about it—the swift attacks, the terror—and what happened to the victims. He was a sturdy boy, independent and brave, but now he crouched in the blackness of the musty-smelling cellar, head in his hands, tears forming in his eyes and sliding down his cheeks.

He wished he could block out the

muffled shots, the screams, the excited whooping from above. The noise frightened him. He was even more frightened when it died away into nothing.

'Pop, Mom,' he whispered. He knew his parents were dead. Otherwise they would have come for him by now. They wouldn't leave him alone in the dark.

Was he going to die too? He tried to remember what Apaches did to any youngsters they caught. Did they torture them to death or did they make slaves of them?

But perhaps it didn't matter. Because then, most frightening of all, came the sound of crackling flames licking at what remained of his home.

TWO

'You've got your orders, Lieutenant, go out to the Reservation, see what's happened and report back here at once. That's all. Dismissed.'

'Yes, sir.' Lieutenant Asa Harrington saluted smartly in reply but Captain Maysfield had already turned his attention to the papers on his desk.

Trying not to sigh, Harrington stepped out on to the porch of Fort Fenton's post headquarters, shading his eyes against the glare of the sun.

He knew Maysfield didn't like him, and had given him this important assignment only in the hope that he would fail.

Although Harrington was twenty-nine and an officer in charge of the men, Maysfield's superior attitude often made him feel awkward and stupid. He told himself he was imagining things and it was his own inferiority complex that was to blame. But he'd learned Maysfield didn't treat the other two lieutenants on the post in the same way, and he was sure they would be the ones recommended for any promotion.

Asa was tall with broad shoulders and a narrow waist. He had brown curly hair, a neat brown moustache and brown eyes. He'd only ever wanted to be a soldier. His parents, who owned a general store in San Francisco, had worked hard and saved even harder to send him to West Point so he could fulfil his dream. To become an officer.

Knowing how lucky he was—an ordinary boy from an ordinary family—to be accepted at the academy, he'd studied as best he could, graduating third in his class.

The humiliation that started at West Point became even worse when he left for a post in Washington. Both the army hierarchy and his fellow officers felt that someone like him, from such a humble background, should be satisfied with joining the army as a private and, at most, becoming a non-commissioned officer. Instead he was an affront to their considerable dignity; especially as he'd done so well at West Point and later performed his duties without having to admit they were too difficult or to beg for help.

Time and again he was passed over for promotion, often for far less able men. Family connections were more important than ability.

Wanting to repay his parents and feeling that he deserved more, Harrington put in a transfer request to Arizona. Perhaps on the frontier he would find the opportunity to gain that elusive promotion.

What had he expected? He didn't really know.

Fort Fenton had turned out to be just

as tough as Washington. His commanding officer was no better than those back East, his men didn't respect him, other officers made it plain they didn't approve. And Captain Maysfield kept him occupied with more paperwork, saying that that was what Harrington's experience made him good at. Thus he'd spent almost all of his time on the fort, with no chance of proving himself.

Certainly the fort wasn't what Harrington had expected. It was like a dot in the valley, with no walls or gates, just adobe huts for the men, the slightly larger headquarters building, a parade-ground, stables and a couple of corrals. His quarters were at the end of Officers' Row and consisted of one small room, which was poorly furnished and extremely uncomfortable.

Neither was the fort fully manned. It hadn't been thought necessary to have a large force present because the Apaches at San Carlos seldom caused trouble and so the men had little to do. The soldiers spent most of their time on routine patrols, painting the buildings, cultivating vegetable patches and escorting the odd wagon train that needed help.

Until now.

Harrington had been in Arizona exactly six months and this was the first time he'd been involved with hostile Indians. The first time he'd been involved with any kind of Indians.

Apaches.

He remembered reading about their bloodthirsty exploits in his youth. And while some of the stories had doubtless been highly coloured in order to sell newspapers and dime novels, they must have had their origins in fact.

Well this was why he'd joined the army—to fight, to defend the white settlers, not to sit behind an office desk shuffling papers around. Still he wished he didn't feel quite as apprehensive as he did at the thought of going up against hostile Apaches. It wasn't that he feared for his own skin—he'd always known and accepted that risk was part of being a soldier—it was that he feared he would make a fool of himself, be unable to cope with a situation he had no experience of dealing with.

But, maybe, this was his chance to grab some glory, to prove to Captain Maysfield and the men that he could succeed. He mustn't fail. Taking a deep breath he put on his gauntlets and went to join his men.

'Here it comes,' Cliff Kendall said pointing, as round the bend in the road the stagecoach lumbered into view heading for the tiny hamlet where he and Leroy Sweeney waited. He patted the nose of his broken down horse while Sweeney clambered down from the buckboard seat.

''Bout time.' Sweeney spoke gruffly in order to hide his nervousness. His heart was beating heavily. Would Benny be on the stage like he'd promised and would he have forgiven Leroy for what had happened?

At last, in a cloud of choking dust, the stagecoach pulled to a halt in front of the tent saloon. Its door swung open and a young man of about twenty-two climbed down.

'Benny!' Sweeney shouted and hurried forward.

Kendall watched, holding back, not wanting to interfere in the brothers' reunion. Besides he was fed up with hearing about Benny—ever since they'd met, Leroy had done nothing but talk about him and worry about how he was getting on; and it had all got worse during the last few weeks when they were due to meet up again.

Kendall was twenty-seven, short and squat, with mean dark eyes and a scar down the left-hand side of his face from a long ago knife fight, in which his opponent came off much worse. He was strong and knew how to look after himself but that didn't stop him sometimes being scared of Sweeney. They had been partners for a while now and mostly they rubbed along OK but Sweeney's temper was uncertain at the best of times and the man wasn't slow to use the two guns he wore in holsters high on his hips or the knife in his boot. He liked to fight and win.

With Benny's return things were going to be different and Kendall had a feeling they weren't going to work out all that well for him.

Sweeney reached his brother and they hugged one another before he pushed Benny away, saying 'Well, look at you!' then immediately hugging him again. Please, he was thinking, let things between me and Benny be back to normal.

'Hey, Leroy, you sure look fine yourself!'

'Benny, how are you?'

'I'm OK, Leroy.'

'Really?'

'Yeah, really.'

Leroy was twenty-six, tall, thickset and

burly with straggly brown hair. He and Benny were obviously brothers even though at the moment, Benny's hair was still cut prison short. Prison routine and prison food had made him thin and pale, bags under his eyes, and his suit was ill-fitting, hanging on his body as if made for someone much larger.

Poor Benny! Sweeney thought, but everything was about to change. While in the past he'd been quite willing to go along with Kendall's small-time plans, robbing stages and lonely trading stores, for nickels and dimes, now Benny was with him again he'd decided they needed something bigger and better. Something to set themselves up for the future.

'What was it like in prison?'

'Not good.' Now he was out, Benny didn't really want to talk about it.

'I'm sure sorry for what happened.'

'It weren't your fault. It was one of them things.'

Sweeney breathed a sigh of relief He still

felt guilty over what had happened to his little brother, although it was thankfully clear that Benny didn't hold a grudge.

It would be more difficult for Leroy to forgive himself. He'd planned the robbery down near the border and it had gone disastrously wrong. He'd escaped, thanks to the shooting and killing of a deputy sheriff, but Benny had been caught; sentenced to two years in Yuma. A hellhole if ever there was one. An unfair sentence, Sweeney thought angrily, considering Benny's age and the fact that he'd never been in trouble before; or never caught at least.

Now Benny had been released and Leroy wanted to do everything he could to make it up to him.

'What plans have you made?' Benny asked. Sweeney was always making plans. He didn't wait for an answer but suddenly spotting Kendall said, 'Hey, who's this?'

'Cliff Kendall. He's been partnering me. Cliff, this is my brother, Benny.' Sweeney ruffled Benny's short hair.

'Yeah, hi.'

Kendall could feel the waves of jealousy coming off the young man. He was right. Benny was going to cause trouble if he could and Kendall would have to watch his back or he'd be on the end of it. If he had any sense he'd walk away now, let the brothers get on with it. But Cliff had taken as many chances as Leroy in Leroy's latest scheme and he wanted, deserved, his share of the profits. Once he'd got his money he could be off. There were always other men to ride along with.

'You know, Leroy, I could sure do with a drink.' Benny looked longingly at the saloon. 'They don't serve beer in Yuma.' A woman too would be nice, because they sure didn't have women in Yuma.

'Yeah, OK, Benny, in a minute. First off I wanna show you something.'

'What?'

'Come here. You asked me if I had any plans, well, Benny, I sure do. I've got a

21

plan that's gonna make our fortune. Ain't that right, Cliff?'

'So you say.'

Sweeney frowned at the other man. 'It's gonna be enough for that stake to start a new life somewhere. Come and look.' He led the way over to the buckboard, the rear of which was covered by a heavy tarpaulin.

'Well?' Benny said impatiently, thinking about beer and women.

Making sure no one was watching, Sweeney flipped back the tarpaulin.

Benny peered under it.

Guns!

THREE

'Sergeant, tell the men to stop here and then come with me.'

'Yes, sir.'

Harrington waited while Sergeant Johnson relayed his orders to the troop of cavalrymen then kicked his horse forward. Immediately the men started moaning about being left out in the middle of the hot, treeless plain. But they were old hands and didn't need anyone to warn them to keep their eyes open and their hands near their guns.

'Looks quiet now, sir.' Johnson was a grey-haired, grizzled old campaigner who recognized his lieutenant's uncertainty and was contemptuous of it.

Harrington looked down at the headquarters of the Indian Agent in charge of the San Carlos Indian Reservation. One or two Apaches in the uniform of the Tribal Police Force patrolled the areas in front of the house and the storage barn. Some old women with empty eyes sat in the scant shade of the corral poles. Otherwise it was deserted. No workers, no horses, no children or dogs running around.

In wary silence the Indians allowed him and Johnson through on to the porch of the house.

As they got there the door opened. Agent Peter Parkin came out. It was his panic-stricken message to Captain Maysfield that was the reason for Harrington bringing the patrol out here. 'Thank God you've arrived! At last! Come in!'

Was there implied criticism in the man's words? But Harrington knew Maysfield had acted as soon as he received the message and the troop couldn't have got here any quicker.

Escaping the hot June sun, they went into the cool room that served as Agent

Parkin's office. The only light came from a small window on the shady side of the building. Through the gloom, Harrington saw someone sitting on the hard chair by a battered filing cabinet. It took him a few moments to recognize Black Feather.

He'd heard a lot about the Indian. In his younger days Black Feather had been a celebrated war chief of the White Mountain Apaches and was still a spokesman for his tribe; as such he was a thorn in the side of the US Army.

'Everything seems peaceful enough.'

'It's quiet, now. Thank God the Tribal Police remained loyal. If it hadn't been for them, more of the bucks might have taken it into their heads to run off. They might even have attacked me and my staff.'

'What happened?'

'It was two nights ago. Twenty or so young men decided to leave. They took some weapons and horses with 'em.'

'Where did they get them from?'

'The horses from us here. You can see

that the corral is empty. The weapons.' Parkin shrugged. 'Who knows? The Apaches are meant to give up their weapons on arrival here but I know, and Maysfield knows, that that doesn't always happen. Normally it's not worth making a fuss over.'

'Your attitude means hostiles are out there now, somewhere, with weapons, prepared to cause trouble,' Harrington said angrily. 'And the settlers won't be expecting it. They won't be ready. They'll be taken by surprise.'

'Unless you catch them first.' Parkin didn't sound very hopeful.

'Why did they go?'

'Trouble's been boiling up for some time. Conditions here aren't perfect by any means. The Apaches are bored. They have nothing to do but spend all their time drinking tiswin or gambling.'

'I thought you were meant to turn them into farmers.'

Parkin shrugged again. 'Even if they

wanted to farm, which they don't, the land they're meant to till isn't suitable. It's too poor. Nothing grows here. And that means there isn't enough to eat because the Indians aren't supposed to hunt for food.'

'But you allow them to, don't you?' Harrington accused. 'Why else would they need to keep their weapons?'

'I let them if it means a difference between them starving or eating, yes.'

'They wouldn't starve. They receive food from the government.'

'Lieutenant, have you seen the rations I have to hand out?'

'Er...no.'

'The rations cause the most trouble of all. They never arrive on time, there's never enough and what there is is often bad. You can hardly blame the Indians for getting angry when they have no food to put in their families' bellies nor for wanting to do something about it.'

'I can't condone anyone breaking the law.'

'Your law, Lieutenant,' the voice came from the corner where Black Feather spoke for the first time. 'Not necessarily ours.'

Harrington stared at him surprised that he'd been able to understand all that was said. But Black Feather spoke good English. It was one more weapon in his fight against the white man.

The Indian got to his feet, his black, hard eyes narrowing. He was slightly taller than Harrington's six feet and lean, with grey streaks in his long black hair. He wore moccasins, a breech-clout and a fringed buckskin shirt. A single eagle's feather, black, dangled from his hair. There was controlled anger in his body as if he held in his temper with some difficulty.

'What happens will be the fault of your so-called just law,' he continued. 'A law that keeps us imprisoned on the poorest land where, as Agent Parkin himself admits, nothing grows. Nothing can live. Why should we be kept here against our will when this was our land in the beginning...?'

'I didn't come here to argue politics,' Harrington interrupted causing Black Feather's eyes to flash and his lips to thin. 'I didn't make the law but I have to abide by it and do my best to defend it. I came here to do my duty. And if you know where these runaways might go then it is *your* duty to tell me so I can prevent trouble.'

'I suppose, Lieutenant, you mean trouble for the whites?'

'In the end it will be your people who suffer the most.'

'Don't you think I know that?'

'Then why didn't you try to stop what happened? I understood you were a great chief whom the bucks took notice of. Or have you lost all your powers?'

'Lieutenant,' Agent Parkin protested.

'Not quite all my powers,' Black Feather said, just as incensed as Harrington by their exchange. 'Hasn't it occurred to you, Lieutenant, that maybe I too would like one more chance to go on the warpath?'

'Then I'd have to come after you and catch you as well.'

'You could try.' And with this the Indian pushed by Harrington and went out of the door letting in a momentary glimpse of the hot sunlight outside.

There was an uncomfortable silence in the agent's office before Parkin shook his head and said, 'You shouldn't have annoyed him.'

'I only spoke the truth.'

'Black Feather doesn't like the idea of the young bucks starting a fight they can't win. He could be a valuable ally on our side.'

'It didn't appear like that to me.'

'But, Lieutenant, you don't know Indians very well do you? Treat Black Feather right he can be a good friend. Treat him badly and he can still be a powerful enemy.'

Harrington thrust his face close to the agent's. 'That's the damn trouble with all you people. You do everything you can to help the Indians when all they want to do is stab us in the back. And then you have to rely on the army to get you out of the mess you've created. When will you learn that force is the only thing they understand?'

Asa was so angry because he knew he'd been wrong to speak to Black Feather as he had, because of which the situation had slipped further out of his control. But he didn't appreciate anyone else pointing out that fact to him, especially in front of his sergeant. Doubtless further knowledge of his ignorance in the handling of Indian affairs would be all over the barracks by nightfall. It might even reach the ears of Captain Maysfield.

The trouble was he *didn't* have any idea how to behave towards or treat the Apaches, whether to be stern or friendly, to consider them as fellow human beings or as wild animals.

But having stated his opinion, to change it now would mean losing face, and one of the first lessons he'd learned at West Point had been never to risk that happening.

Outside he hit his gauntlets against the palm of his left hand while Sergeant Johnson kept his eyes firmly fixed in front of him. Harrington could feel waves of contempt and, worse, pity, coming off of the other man.

As they went over to their horses, Johnson said, 'What are you going to do now, sir?'

Harrington didn't reply but asked a question of his own. 'Why do you think those bucks broke out now? What's stirred them up more than usual?' It wasn't right for a lieutenant to ask his sergeant such questions but Johnson had been on the frontier for so long that he knew Apaches and their ways as well as any soldier could.

Johnson kept the surprise at his lieutenant's question out of his voice as he said, 'Well, sir, I'd say that mebbe they're going to get hold of some guns from somewhere.'

'They've already got weapons.' Harrington wondered what the sergeant was talking about.

'No, I mean other guns, rifles too.'

'Really?'

'Yes, sir. Before we left the fort there were rumours that renegade gunrunners were operating in the area.'

Harrington frowned, trying to conceal the fact that this was news to him. He wondered how a sergeant had heard those rumours when he, a lieutenant, hadn't. Was he the only one at the fort kept in ignorance?

He hadn't been there as long as everyone else and as an officer he was naturally aloof from the men, and while not coming from the same class as the other officers was not accepted by them either. But did that mean he had to be excluded from fort scuttlebutt and so made to look a fool?

'Where do these gunrunners get their guns?' Again he put aside pride in the hope of information. 'Have we any idea about that?'

'No, sir.'

Harrington debated whether or not to try to find out more for himself. By the time they got back to the other men, he'd decided against it. Captain Maysfield didn't like any of his officers using their initiative; he certainly wouldn't approve of Harrington doing so. Instead he'd take the safe course and do what Maysfield had ordered and go back to the fort and report on what he'd found.

FOUR

When the troop got back to the fort, Captain Maysfield's orderly of the day hurried over to tell Harrington his attendance was requested immediately in the office. The only other person present was the army scout, Fred Ulsen. Ulsen, who lived by his own rules and had no time for protocol, was about Harrington's only friend on the post. Now he managed to send Harrington a look of warning. It meant the captain was in a tricky mood.

'Well, Lieutenant, what did you learn?' Maysfield made it sound as if he thought it would be a miracle if Harrington had discovered anything. He didn't ask Harrington to sit down, although Ulsen was sprawled in a chair in front of the desk, his long legs clad in fringed buckskin trousers stretched out in front of him.

Ulsen always wore buckskins and moccasins and with his hair worn long and braided looked more like an Indian than a white man. Rumours abounded that he'd spent some of his younger days in an Apache camp, although no one was sure if he'd been forced into captivity by the Indians or had joined them willingly. Certainly he knew the land and was able to track it as well as any Apache. He could also speak their language and understood their ways.

Kept standing to attention, red with annoyance at the slight, Harrington said stiffly, 'Sir, some twenty young bucks have gone from the Reservation. They have horses and they're armed. Evidently Agent Parkin lets them keep their weapons.'

If Harrington expected Maysfield to be as annoyed as he was about both that and Parkin's inability to control the situation, he was disappointed.

The captain said, 'On the whole, Parkin

is a good man. Unfortunately he's trying to do his job in a situation that is difficult at best and impossible most of the time. And once an Indian gets an idea in his head it's hard to stop him from doing what he wants. Of course, you wouldn't know that, Lieutenant, but I'm right aren't I, Fred?'

'Yes, sir. An Indian can be almighty stubborn when he likes.'

'What else?'

'It appears they're going to buy more weapons from some gunrunners who are operating in the territory. At least, Sergeant Johnson says he's heard rumours to that effect.'

'Ah, Sergeant Johnson, yes. A good man.' Clearly Maysfield thought Johnson, not Harrington, was the brains behind the troop. 'What do you think, Fred?'

'They're the rumours.'

'Sir, what I don't understand is how the Apaches knew these renegades had guns and when to break out. How do they know where to meet them?'

'Ah, Lieutenant, who can say? The Apaches are a law unto themselves and have all manner of ways of communicating information about which we're completely ignorant.'

Ulsen added, 'Well if the bucks do get their hands on guns there'll be no stopping 'em until a lot of damage has been done.'

'Stop them we must.' Maysfield thumped his desk with one fist then turned to a map of the area, which hung on the wall behind him.

It showed an almost empty country of desert and mountains, crisscrossed by lonely roads and dotted with isolated ranches and tiny settlements. Ideal country for Indian warfare, where the Apaches, skilled in travelling long distances without needing much water, knowing the land and living off it, could run and hide; while the army, on its grain-fed horses, tried to follow but often ended up going round in circles, men and horses dead on their feet.

And there, not far away, was the border with Mexico across which the Indians could flee when they were ready, knowing only too well that the army couldn't pursue them.

'To stop the hostiles and return them to the Reservation must be our main concern. But we must also find and catch the gunrunners. Bring them to justice. After all the Indians are acting out of a feeling of frustration and helplessness over their situation. The gunrunners are acting out of greed. Fred, have you any idea where a meeting between them will take place?'

'No, sir. It could be anywhere. But, myself, I reckon it'll be near the border.'

'I agree. Of course we both might be wrong. And unfortunately there's a lot of land to cover.' Maysfield rubbed his chin with his hand, sounding thoughtful.

Harrington wasn't fooled. He had the feeling that the man had already made up his mind what he was going to do, and that it wasn't going to be anything in Asa's favour.

'We haven't much time. Fred, I want you to go out, down around Tucson, see what you can find there. Lieutenant, you go in the other direction towards the mountains.'

'Which troop shall I take? Sergeant Johnson...'

'You'll be taking no one.'

'You want me to go on my own?' Harrington asked, surprised.

'Yes. You're a reasonably good tracker and...'

'Me, sir?'

'Yes, you sir! Are you questioning my orders or my judgement, Lieutenant?'

'No, sir.'

'I'm so glad to hear that. All I want you, both of you, to do is try to find the tracks of either the Indians or the gunrunners. That doesn't require a troop. I want the men here ready to respond to whichever of you has luck and also to protect the stage routes and the citizens who might come into the fort. Does that meet your approval, Lieutenant?'

'Yes, sir.'

'Good. There's no time to waste. This is urgent. Leave straightaway.'

Harrington saluted, aware of the smug look of satisfaction on the face of his commanding officer. The man wasn't only sending him out to confront possible danger alone but in the sure knowledge that he'd fail.

'Don't worry about it, Asa,' Ulsen said, as they left the office and emerged into the harsh afternoon sunlight.

Across the way some of the men were being put through rifle drill by a bored looking corporal. It was a pointless exercise as they knew what to do. From the direction of the stables came the ring of the blacksmith's hammer. Otherwise the place was quiet.

'But I'm not a tracker,' Harrington objected. 'I don't know the first thing about following a trail. Maysfield knows that too.'

'Myself I think I'll find the trail over near Tucson. But in case I'm wrong you be careful. Don't go acting the hero and tackle any one on your own. Getting a posthumous promotion won't do you much good.'

'All right,' Harrington said, not expecting to find anything anyway. And quite sure that after all this he would remain a lieutenant for the rest of his army career.

FIVE

The wagon creaked slowly across the brown sand of the desert valley towards the low line of distant foothills.

Sweeney was driving, Benny sitting beside him. Cliff Kendall rode his horse by their side. They were all alone; the land was devoid of people or animals.

'How much longer d'you think?' Benny asked, wiping a hand across his lips. 'We seem to have been travelling forever. It's hot and I'm thirsty. I didn't have time for but one beer in that saloon.' He glanced slyly across at Kendall. The older man didn't like him or his whining, so naturally he whined all the more. 'I could do with a gal too. You wouldn't let me have one.'

'Shouldn't be much longer,' Sweeney said. 'I'm sorry I couldn't let you stop

43

any longer in that saloon, Benny, but we had to be on our way. The bucks are up ahead somewhere in those hills. They're expecting us, we couldn't keep 'em waiting.'

'They won't hurt us, will they?'

'Not scared are you, Benny?' Kendall sneered.

'"Course I ain't,' Benny said angrily.

'"Course he ain't.' Sweeney scowled. 'Ain't no reason to be scared. We've got what the bucks want, ain't we? They ain't likely to do us any harm.'

Which, Kendall thought, showed how little Leroy knew about Indians, Apaches in particular.

'Don't look so worried. I know what I'm doing.'

'I hope so,' Kendall muttered and urged his horse on ahead of the wagon, scared that if he remained near Benny he'd punch the young man in the face. So far he hadn't dare do so; Leroy would go up against him for it. It was a wonder to him how

Leroy, so smart in so many ways, was fooled by his brother, thinking him so wonderful while Kendall thought it was a pity Benny wasn't still in prison; it was where he belonged.

The further into this empty land they travelled the more Kendall regretted his agreeing to go along. Sweeney was only doing all this to get a stake for himself and Benny and no argument of Kendall's had persuaded him otherwise. This was hardly the first time he'd questioned Leroy's sometimes ambitious ideas but once the man's mind was made up you went along with him or faced the consequences.

And Kendall had to admit that in the past things had usually worked out all right. But now they were venturing into Apache territory. And who knew what Indians might take it into their heads to do? Or what Leroy and Benny had in mind for him once they'd got their money?

'Cliff looks real unsure about all this,' Benny said.

'Aw hell I don't know why.' Sweeney himself was sure gunrunning to the Apaches contained little or no risk to themselves especially as it had been so easy to set up. All he'd had to do was drop the word to one or two of the older Apaches who hung around Tucson and rely on them to take it back to the Reservation.

It still amazed him how soon Red Lance, a well-known trouble-maker, had got in touch with him. When he was persuaded that Sweeney could sell him guns, it hadn't been difficult for the Indian to get several of the other young and reckless bucks so worked up they broke out of San Carlos.

As far as Sweeney could see the only trouble might come from the army but he didn't have much time or respect for the soldiers. By the time they found out what was happening and where, both the Indians and the gunrunners would be long gone.

It was working out perfectly...

Except for Cliff Kendall. Kendall didn't

approve of the scheme and, although he didn't dare say so, Sweeney had the feeling he didn't approve of Benny.

'You know,' Benny leant towards him and said quietly, trying to cause more trouble, 'Cliff is always saying you're taking us into danger but I bet he'll be more 'n happy to grab his share of the money. He'll approve then all right. Mebbe you should split up from Cliff. Just you and me, Leroy? That'd be good wouldn't it?'

'Yeah I guess. But it'd be a shame.' Kendall had always been a good partner. But it was a fact the man was starting to get on Sweeney's nerves. He didn't have any vision, that was his problem. He was content to remain a small-time outlaw; Sweeney wasn't.

'But I come first, don't I? And if there was only the two of us we wouldn't have to split the money up so many ways.' Benny paused to let this sink in then went on, 'And, Leroy, I'm real fed up with all his moaning about you and your ideas. He does nothing but complain. Behind your back anyhow.'

'What's he been saying 'bout me?'

'He said it was only a piece of luck that you didn't end up dead or in jail in Tucson. And that what happened was all your fault. Just because that trader nearly caught you while you were robbing him.'

'He said all that did he?' Sweeney scowled.

'Yeah. I shut him up though. I said I didn't like him talking that way 'bout you. I know it coulda happened to anyone. You had to shoot the trader, didn't you, Leroy? He didn't give you any choice. And it weren't your fault either that a posse started after you.'

Sweeney smiled affectionately at Benny.

'Listen to him and you'da thought you nearly got caught on purpose. But I know you wouldn't do that, especially not after what happened to me when I was caught by the law.'

Sweeney reddened, not liking to be

reminded of that. He stared at Kendall's back where the man rode up ahead. He was tempted to shoot him there and then but, although he was convinced there wouldn't be any trouble with the Apaches, a third gun might come in handy, just in case. Afterwards though...

Then it was too late.

Kendall came galloping back towards them. 'Look!' He pointed ahead of him.

'Jesus,' Benny whispered, his heart beginning to hammer in his chest.

In a cleft in the foothills several mounted Indians had appeared. At the same time three or four more rode out from the rocks, galloping towards the wagon, their yipping clearly heard on the still desert air.

SIX

Asa Harrington rode slowly and cautiously up the steep grassy slope. He was a day's ride away from Fort Fenton and, so far, had spotted no sign of the renegade Indians. But now, on the far side of the hill, a steady spiral of smoke rose up into the still air. Of course it could be from a kitchen stove or some cowboys' camp-fire but he didn't think so and he was taking no chances.

Drawing his rifle from its scabbard he lay it across the saddle in front of him. He was aware that his heart was beating uncomfortably fast and his mouth had become suddenly dry.

As he reached the rim no Indians came out from the rocks to challenge him. They had been here though.

The burnt remains of what had once been a substantial farm lay in the valley below. Little remained, only some piles of charred and still smouldering wood and the broken-down walls of a horse corral.

So Fred Ulsen was wrong when he said the hostiles would head for the border. They'd come this way. But where were they now? From the state of the house it seemed to Harrington that the attack had taken place a couple of days before and the Indians were likely long gone. In case he was wrong he remained where he was, eyes searching the rocks and undergrowth in front of him.

Suddenly something came crashing out of the bushes towards him. Instantly he swung round in the saddle, brought up his rifle and fired. Then leant forward, breathing fast and trying to smile as he saw that his would-be assailant was a deer, as scared of him as he'd been startled by it. It sprang around and took to its heels, bounding away.

Well, Harrington thought wryly, at least there's nothing wrong with my reflexes.

The shot had brought no sign of life from anywhere around and thinking himself safe, he dug heels into his horse's side, starting down towards the burnt house.

In the yard, he dismounted and, still clutching the rifle, saw that quite a fight had taken place here. There was evidence of dried blood and the marks of a body being dragged away but he thought the defenders' stand had probably been short lived. They wouldn't have been expecting trouble. The odds against them were overwhelming.

He was sure he was right when he found the two bodies—a man and a woman. Mercifully for the woman it looked as if the man had killed her with a quick clean shot to the head before they were overcome. A pity he hadn't had time to do the same for himself. He'd clearly been tortured before being allowed to die, then scalped.

Harrington swallowed hard against the sick feeling in his stomach. Reading about

Indian depredations wasn't exactly the same as witnessing their aftermath.

Hard work was the answer. The couple couldn't just be left where they had fallen. Once the wood had stopped smoking they would be the prey of wild animals and buzzards. He would have to bury them.

The earth was hard and he decided not to dig down very far but to cover the graves with stones and hope that way they wouldn't be disturbed. He had almost finished when he heard a noise from somewhere behind him.

'Shit!' he muttered and dived for his rifle. Nothing. Harrington knew he was jittery but surely he wasn't that scared he'd started to imagine things.

No! There it was again. A sort of tapping noise. Perhaps it was the wood settling.

'Help.'

The voice was so faint that, for a moment, Harrington thought he'd imagined that as well. Then he heard it once more.

It came from the burnt house.

Surely no one could have survived the fire and no one would be hiding amongst the still hot ruins, but most of these places had cellars in which to store food and in which to hide in case of attack. Pulling on his gauntlets, Asa started to pull the wood away. The tapping noise was a little louder now, and soon he could tell from which direction it came.

Finally dragging some more burnt planks to one side, he saw a trapdoor. In the middle was an iron ring.

Catching hold of it, wincing because it was still hot, Harrington pulled. Nothing happened. It was stuck. He pulled harder and reluctantly the trapdoor came up, revealing a set of steps leading down into the darkness. And crouched on one of them, near the top, was a boy of about ten, who peered fearfully up at him, blinking in the sudden light.

'It's all right,' Asa said as calmly as he could.

'Apaches,' the boy whimpered.

'They've gone. You're safe. Here.' Harrington reached out a hand. 'Come on, son. There's no danger. Let me help you out of there.' The boy clutched his hand and climbed out into the open, blinking again, but this time in disbelief as he saw what little remained of his home. Harrington was glad that the bodies of the man and woman, obviously his parents, were out of sight.

The boy had corn-coloured hair, now untidy and dirty, and blue eyes. Tears had tracked lines down his cheeks. He looked badly frightened, which was understandable, and clung to Asa's hand as if he would never let go.

Harrington hunkered down in front of him. 'What's your name, son?'

The boy didn't reply and Harrington was scared that the shock of the attack had caused him to forget who he was, then he whispered. 'Timmy O'Brien.'

'Do you know how long you were in the

cellar?'

'A long time.'

'Did you see who did this?'

'Apaches. They attacked just as I was getting up. I could hear them yelling. I was very scared. Was it wrong to be scared?'

'No, of course, it wasn't. I would have been scared as well.'

'Would you?'

'Yes. Are you hungry, thirsty?'

Timmy nodded.

'Come with me then.' Keeping himself between Timmy and his dead parents, Harrington led him over to his horse. He handed the boy the canteen of water. 'Here, take a sip or two. Later I'll cook us some bacon and beans. Would you like that?' He was reluctant to light a fire when the Indians might see it but thought he ought to make an exception in this case. The boy needed and might feel better for something hot to eat.

'Sir? Where's Pop and Mom?'

It was the question Harrington was

dreading. He put his arm round the boy's shoulders. There was no point in lying. 'I'm sorry, Timmy, they're both dead. They died quickly and didn't suffer beforehand.' Or at least Mrs O'Brien hadn't and Timmy didn't need to know about his father. 'You must be brave. They died for you, so you could live.'

Timmy sank to the ground and began to cry.

Helplessly Harrington watched him, knowing he could do nothing for him. Leaving him to his grief he went back to digging the graves. It was hot work and he was covered with sweat by the time he'd finished burying the bodies. He wished he could fashion a couple of crosses to put on the graves but he had neither the tools nor the time. All he could do was say a few words over the O'Briens.

As he stood there, head bowed, praying, he was aware of Timmy by his side, reaching again for his hand.

And Timmy was another problem. What

exactly was he going to do with him? Harrington didn't know anything about small boys or how to treat them. Obviously he couldn't be left out here alone but Captain Maysfield would hardly appreciate it if Harrington returned to the fort so soon after he'd started out.

'Timmy, my name is Asa Harrington. I'm a lieutenant at Fort Fenton. Do you know where that is?'

'Yes, sir.'

'I'm on a special mission for my commanding officer. Would you like to come along? You can ride behind me on my horse.'

'Where are you going?'

'Into the hills.'

'Is that where the Apaches are?'

'Maybe. I don't know. They could have gone by now.'

For a moment Timmy looked frightened again but with a determined tilt of his head, he said, 'I'll come along.'

SEVEN

The Sweeneys and Cliff Kendall were led deep into the hills by the Apaches. Not a word was said by the Indians as they rode ahead, behind and all round the wagon, those in front pausing now and again to make sure it was still following them.

'I don't like this,' Kendall muttered, leaning down towards Leroy. 'They could be taking us anywhere. How do we know we can trust 'em? They might just take the guns and kill us.'

'Now who's the coward?' Benny said under his breath. But he felt much the same way, his palms slicked with sweat, a sick feeling in the pit of his stomach.

Only Sweeney seemed at ease. 'Of course we can trust 'em,' he said impatiently. 'They want guns, we've got 'em. They don't treat us right no one else will trade with 'em ever again.'

Which wouldn't exactly help them if they were dead, Kendall thought sourly.

It was getting dark, the valley already in deep shadow when the Indians came to a halt in a large clearing amongst the rocks and undergrowth. By the light of a burning fire it was possible to see that more Indians awaited them there.

Sweeney pulled the wagon to a halt and climbed down. Despite his confident air, his legs felt shaky. He'd never been this close to wild Apaches before. He was sure that what he said was right, that if the Apaches wanted more weapons they'd hardly kill the traders who could provide them but supposing they took it into their unpredictable heads to test the weapons before buying them...?

'Come on,' he said turning to Benny. 'Let's get this over with. And for Chrissakes, the pair of you, start acting like you ain't got a care in the whole damn world.'

Smile plastered on his face, flanked by his two companions, Sweeney approached the fire.

The Indians who had met them and brought them here, dismounted and joined the others fanning out behind a tall, older man. He didn't look particularly happy at the excitement around him.

'Christ! That's Black Feather!' Kendall said in Sweeney's ear. 'What the hell is he doing here?'

Everyone knew Black Feather's old reputation. His new one had him working for peace. It didn't look like that was true, not if the wily old fox was here, ready to buy guns.

Sweeney was suddenly as worried as Kendall. He'd expected to deal with the young and inexperienced Red Lance, not with someone like Black Feather. But it was too late to do anything but carry on. Try to turn round and leave would mean instant death and if he looked anything less than confident, the Indians might well suspect something was wrong.

He raised his hand in greeting and said, 'Black Feather, what an honour. We didn't expect to see you here.'

Another Indian stepped forward. Red Lance was only twenty and full of fire. Not only did he hate the authorities but having been forced on the Reservation when he was still young had never had the chance to go on the warpath, despite having been raised to expect to fight and kill his enemies. Along with other hotheads he believed that violence was the only way for the Apaches to regain the homeland that had once been theirs. And for that guns were needed.

'My uncle is here because of the way the army treated him at San Carlos but he is here reluctantly because he believes fighting will cause more trouble for us than for the white men who have taken over our land.'

'Not if you have the right weapons,' Sweeney said, hoping that Black Feather wasn't about to persuade his nephew not to buy the guns after all but to give himself up to Agent Parkin. 'With weapons at your side you can get yourself and your people a fairer deal. Without them you're as good as dead. They're the only way to get lasting peace in the region.'

Red Lance looked bored at that; he wasn't concerned with peace only with war.

'Are you not concerned about what will happen to your fellow white man?' Black Feather asked.

'Of course,' Sweeney lied, nodding wisely. 'But we believe that more should be done to honour the Apaches who were here long before the white man.'

'So you are on our side?'

Sweeney hoped the Indian wasn't about to suggest they join him on the warpath and thinking quickly, said, 'We are on the side of right.'

Did a smile cross Black Feather's face? It was obvious to Sweeney that while Red

Lance and the others didn't care what the gunrunners' motives were, Black Feather knew only too well that they were doing this for no other reason than to make a profit. And despised them for it. But would he do anything other than buy the guns and let them leave?

A tremor of some sort rippled through the gathered Indians and Red Lance turned to his uncle and spoke rapidly in Apache. None of the white men knew what he said but after a while Black Feather nodded and stood aside.

'My uncle has agreed that we can go ahead.'

Sweeney tried not to sigh with relief. 'In that case perhaps you'd like to inspect the guns?'

The Apaches swarmed round the wagon, lifting the tarpaulin. A collective sigh of excitement went up from them as they saw the weapons—rifles and revolvers—packed in the wagonbed, row upon row of them. While Black Feather and Red Lance looked on, some of the bucks took hold of the guns, pulling them out to examine them more closely.

Sweeney had very carefully made sure that none of them was loaded, the ammunition being kept separately.

'So far so good,' he said to Benny as the Indians jabbered amongst themselves, hefting the weapons in the air, peering along the sights, pulling the triggers. 'Come on, Red Lance,' he urged under his breath, 'pay what you owe us and let us get outa here.'

'Look,' Kendall nudged him.

From somewhere drink had been produced: bottles of cheap whiskey, beer, tiswin. As the drink was passed from hand to hand interest in the guns waned.

'Good. Let the silly bastards get drunk and they won't be able to come after us.'

Like a ghost Black Feather appeared at their sides, making them jump. Sweeney hoped he hadn't heard what he said.

'Everything appears all right,' the Indian spoke gravely.

'I'm sure glad to hear that,' Sweeney replied. 'You won't be disappointed.'

'I hope not.'

'See here, Black Feather, it seems like the celebrations are goin' to go on long into the night.' Sweeney nodded at the bucks who were already squabbling amongst themselves about whose turn it was to take a drink. 'We've got places to go, people to see. How about you order one or two of your men who are still sober enough to unload the guns, you give us the furs we agreed on and we get on our way?'

'Is there any reason for your hurry?'

'No, of course not.' Sweeney hoped sweat didn't break out on his forehead. 'Like I said we just wanna be on our way.'

'Where are you going?'

'Tucson,' Sweeney lied.

'Very well.' Black Feather went back to the Indians and after a few moments of arguing Red Lance and a couple of the others began to unload the buckboard. The Sweeneys and Kendall watched, their eyes alight as several packhorses, loaded with furs, were led into the firelight.

'I hope these will be satisfactory,' Black Feather said.

'Oh I'm sure they will.' Sweeney tried to keep the greed out of his voice.

It didn't take long for the furs to be placed in the wagon. It took even less time for the three white men to leave the campsite. They didn't look back as they left the fire and the drunken revels going on round it.

'Why are we goin' to Tucson?' Benny asked. 'I thought that's where you stole the guns.'

'Of course we ain't goin' there. I just said that in the hope that if the Apaches follow us it might put 'em off our trail for a while.'

Kendall thought that was unlikely knowing how clever the Apaches were at tracking. But even he was in too elated a mood to point this out. Instead, trying hard not to laugh, he said, 'How long do you think it'll be before those poor dumb bastards know they've been fooled?'

Sweeney did laugh. 'Oh, just about as long as it takes for 'em to fire the first gun!'

EIGHT

Asa Harrington pulled his horse to a halt at the bottom of a slope covered with rocks and scrubby grass. He swung his leg over the cantle and slid to the ground, reaching for the canteen.

'How much further are we going?' Timmy O'Brien said. His eyes anxiously ranged the hilltop for any sign of the Indians the lieutenant sought.

'I'm not sure, Tim, not far.'

They hadn't seen any more sign of the Apaches, about which Harrington was thankful. Not for himself but because he was now responsible for the boy. But could he yet go back to the fort and tell Captain Maysfield that? Would Maysfield be satisfied or would he expect Harrington to go on until he did find something? And what was happening at the fort and on the Reservation? For all he knew the Indians could have surrendered.

'Here.' He handed Timmy the canteen, watching the boy as he took a drink, thinking that if he had a son he'd want him to be like Tim.

He admired the boy very much for Timmy was doing his best to be brave and he never complained, not even when they rode for miles and he must have been worn out. Instead he rode behind Harrington on the horse, clinging to his waist, and when they stopped he drank water and ate cold rations, without wishing for anything else.

And at night, even when it turned cold, he said nothing but lay wrapped up in a thin blanket beside the tiny fire, which was all Harrington dare light for fear that Indians were still in the vicinity and would spot anything larger.

Sometimes Asa heard him crying in the dark, but not knowing what to say to comfort him left the boy alone. Nothing he could do would bring Timmy's parents back.

'There's a stagecoach road just over the hill and a relay station about five or six miles along it. Let's make sure the folks there are OK and then we'll go back to the fort. All right?'

'Yeah, Lieutenant, all right. Lieutenant?'

'Yes?'

'What's going to happen to me when we do reach Fort Fenton?'

'Tim, have you got any relatives you could go to?'

The boy thought for a moment or two then shook his head. 'I don't think so. Not out here in Arizona anyway. My mom's family came from Ohio but I don't know about Pop's.'

Harrington squeezed Timmy's arm. 'Never mind. Let's worry about it when we have to. I expect Captain Maysfield will know what to do.'

'What can I tell you, Mr Ulsen?' Midge

71

Draper said. 'Everyone round here knows the guns I sell ain't up to much. Most of 'em are pre-Civil War models and are so old and worn out they don't work too well. Half the time you can't get ammunition for 'em. Mebbe I should take more precautions, have better locks on the doors but, hell, up till now it ain't seemed worth the bother.'

Ulsen sighed and took a swig of the warm beer the weapons trader had given him. He felt unhappy being within Tucson's town limits. The place was hot and dusty. Busy too. Wagons blocked the street outside the small store, men and women wandered up and down the sidewalks. The clamour of hammering and sawing reached his ear as new buildings went up all over.

He looked round the store, which had a dingy, dilapidated air. Draper probably didn't do much business—who wanted poor weapons, except collectors or those who either didn't know anything about guns or who couldn't afford anything better? Somehow the gunrunners had not only found out about the guns but also that the locks wouldn't keep them out. It probably hadn't been difficult. Draper didn't look the type to keep quiet about his business. The robbers had then decided to make a double profit by not paying for the guns they were about to sell.

'So, what happened?'

'What happened was that me and my wife were asleep upstairs. She woke me up, said she'd heard a noise. I thought she was imagining things but to satisfy her I came down to see. There were two men in here and they had a buckboard outside.'

'Did you see 'em clearly?'

Draper shook his head. 'The moon was bright that night but not that good. I couldn't make anything out but that they were both white, young and rough looking. Besides I'd no sooner said something like "Hey, what are you doing?" before one of the bastards turned round and shot me.' He indicated his arm, which was in a sling. 'My wife screamed, the other one said, "We've got enough let's get outa here" and they ran outside. One drove the buckboard away, the other rode a horse.'

'Did anyone else hear any of this?'

'Not in time to stop 'em. Some people came running from the saloons. It was too late and dark to go after 'em but in the morning the marshal started out with a posse.'

'Didn't have any luck I suppose?'

'Nope. Lost 'em in the rocks. Reckon myself that once the posse got near to where they thought the wild bucks might be waiting they turned back. Can't say I blame 'em none.'

'Which way did the robbers go? Towards the border?'

'Nope.'

Ulsen was surprised. 'Are you sure?'

'Yeah. The posse followed 'em for quite a-ways. They seemed to be heading for the Wickenburg Mountains. It's pretty empty country up that way, although there are one or two ranches and small towns. And the stage goes that way too. But I shouldn't worry too much about the Apaches causing trouble. Those guns won't help 'em in whatever grievance they think they've got.'

'Oh?'

'Like I said most of the guns I've got here want a lot of work done on 'em before they can be fired.'

'And the ones stolen were the same?'

'That's right. Those Indians line someone up in their sights and they pull the trigger, poof, ain't nothing gonna happen.'

Ulsen left the store and stood for a moment on the sidewalk, wondering what to do. The fact that the Indians had got their hands on more or less worthless weapons was something to be thankful for. But it didn't do a lot to ease his main worry: which was that as the gunrunners had gone towards Wickenburg, so the Indians must have done too.

There they would do their trade; guns

for furs the Indians would have stockpiled from past hunts in the event that an opportunity like this came their way.

And the Wickenburg Mountains was where Lieutenant Asa Harrington had gone. All by himself.

'There's the stage road, Tim.' Harrington looked down the hill to the narrow trail that snaked its way across the desert. 'The relay station should be that way.' He pointed eastwards. 'Are you tired, Tim?'

'Yeah a bit.'

'We can rest up there for a while. They'll have hot food and a bed.'

Safety too.

NINE

'Don't go too far,' Doug Watts called out to his daughter as she went out of the door.

'Don't worry, I'm only going to water the vegetables. I'll be careful.' Rose tried not to sigh. There were still times when her father treated her like a child. She was twenty now, almost twenty-one, and she knew enough not to take risks at any time, let alone when there was the possibility of an attack by Indians, remote though that seemed.

Collecting a bucket of water from the well she carried it down the slope to the small garden she cultivated each year. She sprinkled the water over the few vegetables that were endeavouring to push their way up through the barren earth. With her help they stood a slight chance of growing, without it they stood none.

When she'd finished she walked back to the corral, leaning against the adobe wall staring out at the land. It stretched, brown and empty, to each horizon, broken only by a cluster of rocks here and there and, in the distance about half a mile away, the stunted trees that marched along either side of the creek.

The land was always empty but during the last couple of days with Indian trouble in the air it was emptier than usual. Even the stage had stopped running. It stood now in the yard outside the barn and the guard and the driver, Mr Turner and Eddie Robertson, were in the house talking to her father and wondering whether to go on into Wickenburg.

They would have risked it if they'd had any passengers but no one had wanted to make the journey once the news of the latest Apache outbreak had spread.

Watts' Station the place was called. After

her father. He had been put in charge of the stagecoach relay station when it was first built and he'd remained throughout all kinds of dangers and troubles, and good times too.

It was situated at the end of a small range of low hills that petered out near the creek. And gradually over the years it had evolved into a substantial set of buildings: a fair-sized adobe house, with a shaded porch all the way round, a barn, stables, corral and several other outbuildings. Besides the well, there was a small water-hole fed by the creek; this sometimes dried up in the summer, although the well never did.

Doug Watts was considered a good man, reliable, steadfast but sometimes a worrier especially over his motherless daughter.

Rose knew he spent a lot of time wondering if she was growing up as a young lady should, whether she was lonely, or whether for her sake he should sell up and go into town. And she supposed she did sometimes get lonely and envy her friends who had beaux or were already married.

But she liked meeting the people who travelled on the stage, liked the tasks of feeding them and making sure they were provided with clean towels and soap. Best of all here, in the desert, she liked the freedom to do as she pleased; something her friends in Wickenburg knew little about.

Rose was like her father in temperament and looks, being thin and of average height. She had the same fair hair, which she kept cut quite short for convenience, light-grey eyes and a tanned skin from being out in the sun most of the day. She usually wore men's shirts, boots and a divided skirt. And sometimes, if no one was around, she wore pants—they were so much easier when there was work to be done. She never did so if a stage was coming in because there might be a passenger on board who wouldn't approve. However, she was wearing them now because she didn't consider Mr Turner and Eddie visitors for they had known her since she was a child.

And today she had a pistol stuck in the belt at her side. She knew how to use it too, although, she admitted, she was good at target practice, which was a lot different to shooting at a live target. She hoped she could do that too if she had to.

Rose turned as she heard footsteps approaching her.

'You'd better come in now,' Watts said. He was carrying a rifle. 'Just in case.'

'I thought you and Mr Turner had decided the Indians won't be coming this way.'

'I hope they won't.'

'There's no sign of them.'

'That's when you have to be most careful.'

'I hope this scare will soon be over and we can get back to normal,' Rose said as she followed her father. She didn't like being cooped up inside with nothing to do. She liked to be outside getting on with things.

'Me too, Rosie. In the meantime it don't do to take any chances.' Watts knew she wasn't listening. He had a feeling his daughter wasn't taking the situation as seriously as she should.

He was right. Rose wasn't really worried. The house would be easy to defend. It had been built in the days when Indian attacks were much more common and the windows and doors had bars and stout shutters, with loopholes in them from which the defenders could fire without much risk to themselves. Any Apache stupid enough to attack them would soon give up.

Besides she had faced few dangers in her life and those nothing more than a feisty horse or a rattlesnake hiding in the undergrowth—all of which she could handle quite easily and she was sure nothing could or would happen to jeopardize their lives.

Watts, who'd been out here much longer, wasn't so convinced. He'd thought of sending her into town with Mr Turner and Eddie but knew she would never go. He sighed. It was sometimes very difficult being the father of a daughter, especially a strong-willed one.

As they walked up the slope a young man came out of the stables. Nick Manning was nineteen, tall and gangly, with blank brown eyes. He was Watts' latest wrangler and a good, hard worker if a little simple.

Rose waved to him and Watts called, 'Keep a watch out, Nick, and be careful.'

'Sure thing, Mr Watts.'

'Come on in in a few minutes. Food'll be on the table.'

As they reached the house, Rose paused to look back. 'I wish we knew what was happening.'

'Someone will come out from Wickenburg to tell us soon enough. In the meantime all we can do is wait and hope for the best.'

TEN

The Sweeneys and Kendall had made camp in a dip in the hills where their fire wouldn't easily be seen.

Now, while Leroy and Benny hitched up the wagon, Kendall climbed to the top of the ridge where he could look along their back-trail. They hadn't been able to travel far or fast while it was dark but there wasn't any sign of the Indians, who hopefully were still sleeping off their drink and hadn't yet realized the deception.

'Well?' Sweeney looked round as Kendall went back to where the two brothers waited for him.

'Ain't anyone coming after us as far as I can tell. Not yet anyway.'

'I told you we had nothing to worry about,' Sweeney boasted.

Benny climbed up onto the wagon seat beside his brother. 'What we gonna do now, Leroy?'

'Sell these furs.' Sweeney reached round to touch the pile of furs in the wagonbed. 'Then we hightail it outta here as quick as we can towards New Mexico. Perhaps we'll go to Santa Fe. I've heard tell that is a real nice town and we ain't wanted there! You ready, Cliff? Let's go.'

A couple of hours later they'd left the foothills behind and were travelling across the scrubby brown desert. Sweeney knew where he was headed: a place he'd earlier heard about through saloon gossip, and which he thought would be ideal for their purpose. Before long it came into view.

It didn't look up to much. A long, low adobe store, nestling in the shadows cast by the rocky slope of a butte; a pole corral in front, where a few horses foraged, a well and a dug-out with grass growing from the roof.

'Michael Apscott's trading store,' he

announced to his rather surprised companions. 'It's been here for twenty years or so. Apscott makes a living out of trading with cattle ranchers and, as there's usually an Apache squaw and half-breed kids in evidence, he trades safely with the Apaches as well.' Which was how Sweeney knew the man wouldn't have been attacked by Red Lance.

'And he'll buy the furs?' Benny asked.

'From what I hear he buys furs from the Indians, so why shouldn't he buy 'em from us?'

'But he won't pay as much as we'd get if we took 'em to Santa Fe,' Kendall objected.

Sweeney clamped down on the temper he was in danger of losing. Why did Cliff always have to argue with him and find fault with his plans? 'Look, OK, maybe we won't get quite such a good price here but Apscott also has horses for sale.'

'So?' said Kendall.

'So, that means we can trade in our

wagon and these played-out old nags for three fresh animals. With three decent horses and nothin' to slow us down, we've got the means to escape from the Apaches who ain't gonna be any too pleased at how we've cheated 'em. I dunno about you but I'd rather have money in my pocket and a good horse under my knees than be stuck out here with a slow moving wagon piled up with furs.'

Benny looked anxiously over his shoulder as if expecting to see a bunch of angry bucks appearing on the horizon. 'Me too.'

'Honestly, Cliff, do you really expect that the Indians won't come after us, revenge in their hearts, once they find out those guns are no good?'

Kendall sighed, wondering why the hell he'd let Leroy talk him into this crazy scheme.

'We need to be able to ride, and fast, to get out of the area. And the army might be after us by now, although I don't suppose they've got any idea of where we are. All agreed? Good. When we get to the store, just remember we're hunters. We ain't got nothin' to do with guns or Apaches. Right?'

Michael Apscott stood in the entrance to his store, staring out at the wagon and the three men making their way towards him.

He was an old man now, almost seventy, and had been in this land a very long time. He'd originally come out with a caravan of fancy goods on the old Santa Fe Trail, well before the Civil War. He'd been an army scout, a guide for the wagon trains, a buffalo hunter. And, finally, when his rheumatism made riding difficult he'd started this trading store. It didn't make much money but it enabled him to live reasonably comfortably without having to do too much work.

Unlike many of his compatriots, he'd always got along with the Indians. He'd killed a few of them, when it had been a case of kill or be killed; one had given him a knife wound in the side. But he'd actually respected them and taken an interest in their different way of life. He'd learned their customs, learned to speak their language.

He believed it was inevitable that the Apaches would end up on reservations because they were in the way of the tide of a white development that couldn't be stopped. And while he knew that conditions at San Carlos weren't exactly good he thought that with a bit more understanding on both sides they could get better. Now some of the younger bucks had been persuaded to break out. It was a rotten deal all round. In the end it would come out badly for everyone. And worse for the Indians.

He also knew that it was the opportunity of obtaining cheap guns that had caused the trouble.

As the three men came closer, Apscott stared hard at them. He turned back into the store where his latest Indian wife, a woman some thirty years younger than him, was tidying the counter.

'Go in the back,' he ordered.

Sweeney pulled the wagon up close to the store's low doorway. He and Benny got down while Kendall dismounted and stretched. All three sauntered into the store. It was crowded and untidy with goods piled everywhere: furs, farming equipment, barrels of nails, tinned fruit.

Apscott came round the corner of the counter. He'd buckled on a gun and his rifle wasn't far away. 'What can I do for you, gents?'

'Got anything to drink?' Sweeney asked. 'We could sure slake our thirst. It's hot out there.'

'There's water. I don't keep beer or spirits.'

Sweeney didn't believe him but decided not to argue, for the moment. 'We'll fill up our canteens before we go if you don't mind. We'd like to trade. Got some furs outside. Also we want to buy three horses. You look like you've got some good horseflesh out in the corral.' He smiled broadly.

Apscott wasn't fooled by the man's pleasantness; his smile didn't reach his eyes. The trading store might be out in the middle of nowhere but that didn't mean Apscott didn't have all kinds of men stopping by and he was usually adept at recognizing what type they were. These three looked like trouble.

He accompanied them outside and peered in the wagon, surprised at seeing so many furs. 'Where did you get 'em from?'

'Been hunting up in the Wickenburg Mountains,' Kendall replied. 'Leroy, while you dicker over the furs, do you want me to saddle up three horses?'

Sweeney frowned, hoping that the trader didn't pick up on Kendall's anxiety to be on his way. But he nodded his agreement because, after all, he was anxious as well.

'You've got some good furs here,' Apscott admitted. 'You musta been out for quite a while.'

'Several months.'

'You didn't see any Indians up there?'

Benny giggled and Sweeney said, 'We saw sign of 'em. Especially in the last couple of days. Has anything happened we should know about?' he added, trying to sound innocent.

'Some bucks broke out of the Reservation. There are also gunrunners in the area. I suppose you didn't come across them?'

'No, sir.' Sweeney shook his head.

By now Apscott was even more suspicious. These men were acting strangely and they didn't look like hunters to him. Where was their equipment? How could just three of them have got so many furs? 'Wait there,' he said.

Sweeney smirked across at Kendall, who had saddled and bridled three horses, and was leading them round the side of the corral.

'Hell!' Benny suddenly exclaimed.

And as Sweeney looked up the smirk on his face died.

Apscott stood in the doorway, rifle in his hands.

'Hey! What?' Sweeney protested.

'You ain't hunters. You're the god-damned trouble-making gunrunners!'

'Wait a minute, mister!' Kendall protested.

'You get outa here! Right now! This minute! And you leave my horses behind!'

Leroy and Kendall looked at one another in angry surprise.

How had Apscott known? Faced with a man who looked both willing and able to use the gun he carried, they might have done what the trader told them; cut their losses, taken their chances, gone on to Sante Fe.

But events were taken out of their hands. Benny screamed, 'Damn that!' and drawing his gun he aimed it in Apscott's direction and fired.

'Jesus! Benny!' his brother said.

Apscott dived back behind the door, lifting the rifle and returning Benny's fire.

Sweeney and Kendall dived behind the wagon, drawing their own weapons, shooting at the doorway, where the trader crouched. From inside the store they heard a woman cry out.

Rifle bullets kicked up dust round them, the horses whinnied in fright, and Benny used up all the bullets in his gun in quick succession, not hitting anything. He threw the gun down in disgust.

Sweeney aimed carefully. The bullet struck Apscott in the leg, and, with a cry, he fell backwards, dropping the rifle, clutching at his wound.

'Get him! Get him!' Benny yelled. He didn't wait for either of the other two men to act. Grabbing at his gun, he stood up, clawing for more bullets from his cartridge belt.

At the same time one of the store's

windows was flung open and Apscott's Apache wife appeared. She held another rifle and she pulled the trigger.

With a high-pitched scream, Benny clutched at his side and fell down in the dust, almost under the wagon's wheel.

'Benny!' Sweeney cried in horror.

And as Kendall went to shoot at the Apache woman, Apscott drew his revolver and sent several bullets in his direction. Kendall ducked back. This was getting dangerous!

'Let's get Benny outa here!' Leroy yelled.

'With the wagon?'

'Of course with the goddamned wagon! Come on, I ain't got time to argue with you. Benny needs help. For God's sake, Cliff, come on!'

Knowing he would get no further help from Leroy, Kendall raced towards the trader's horses and grabbed the reins of one, hauling himself up into the saddle.

Ignoring the bullets whining round him,

Sweeney went over to where Benny lay on the ground. The boy was wide eyed with pain, holding his side, moaning. Blood seemed to be everywhere. 'Hold on, Benny, hold on! I'll help you!'

'I'm hurting, Leroy! I'm hurting real bad.'

Sweeney picked up his brother's body and as gently as he could, put him in the back of the wagon, nestled amongst the furs. Firing a couple of times at Apscott, he leapt up on to the seat, caught up the reins and urged the horses forward.

Bent low over the horse's back, Kendall rode by him. 'Hell!' he said. 'Now what?'

'I don't know!' Sweeney yelled back. 'Benny's hurt. He's shot. And it's all my fault. We'll have to take him somewhere safe where the bullet can be got out and he can be looked after.'

As far as Kendall was concerned, Benny had brought the trouble on himself, stupid hot-headed bastard that he was! He wanted to suggest that they think of themselves and ditch the young man and let him either die or recover on his own. One glance at Sweeney's distraught face and he wisely decided not to say anything of the sort.

ELEVEN

Asa Harrington rode slowly along the road, holding the rifle across the saddle in front of him. Behind him he could feel Timmy's hands clutching tightly at his belt. He'd been frightened of what he might find at Watts' Station and now that it came into view he was thankful to see that everything looked quiet and peaceful.

As they rode up by the barn, the door to the house opened and several people came out. A man and a girl, alike enough they had to be father and daughter. Two older men and a young man with a vacant look about him.

But Harrington only had eyes for the girl, not because she was the first white girl he'd seen in some time, nor because she was particularly pretty—although she was—but because she had on pants. He'd never seen a girl in pants before, not even a Washington whore, and although he felt he ought to be shocked he actually thought she looked well enough in them.

She must have realized he was staring at her because she went very red but she made no move to get away from his stare; he liked that too.

The man came down from the porch. 'Doug Watts,' he introduced himself. 'Have you come from Wickenburg?'

'No. I'm from Fort Fenton. Lieutenant Asa Harrington.' He raised his hat slightly and dismounted, turning to help Timmy to the ground. 'And this is Timmy O'Brien. His parents have been killed by the Apaches.'

'Oh no, oh the poor boy!' Rose immediately cried.

'Are the Indians on their way?' Watts asked. 'Is that why you're here, to warn us?'

'No,' Harrington shook his head. 'My

captain sent me out several days ago to see what I could find but I haven't seen any sign of the Indians not since I came across Timmy, and that was way down in the foothills.'

'That's something to be thankful for. Why don't you both come inside? We were just about to sit down and eat. You're welcome to join us. Nick, see to the lieutenant's horse.'

'Yes, sir.'

'This is Mr Turner, the stagecoach guard, and Eddie Robertson, the driver. They're here right now because I thought it best the stage stayed put until we got word the routes were safe.'

Mr Turner had brown, balding hair and wary eyes, while Eddie Robertson was slightly older with grey hair and a long grey beard. He smelled of whiskey and cheap cigars. Both men looked fed up with their enforced stay at the stage station.

'And this is Rose, my daughter.'

'Miss Watts,' Harrington said politely, making the girl blush again. 'Come on, Tim, let's go and get something to eat.' And catching hold of Timmy's hand he followed the others inside.

The room which was used by both family and coach passengers was small and dark, lit by only two windows, one on either side of the door. But it was as clean as any place in the middle of the desert could be; just like the Watts's clothes, which were old and patched but washed and neatly pressed. There was a long wooden table at which the passengers sat on benches, eating off tin plates and mugs, while the family's living-quarters was in the far corner, with a couple of comfortable chairs and a table, on which stood a vase containing a few desert flowers.

'I'm afraid it's only stew,' Rose apologized. 'But there's plenty of coffee.'

'It sounds good to me,' Harrington said, sitting down and taking off his hat. 'We've been living off cold rations.'

'Timmy, would you like some lemonade?'

The boy nodded shyly.

'Ah here's Nick. Good. Come on, lad, sit down. Eat up everyone. Rosie, pass the biscuits. Make sure Timmy has enough.'

'Have you had to stay here long?' Harrington asked, addressing Mr Turner and Eddie.

'A couple of days,' Eddie said. 'I guess we could go on, even though Mr Watts says we shouldn't, but there's no one between here and Wickenburg and it's a long way if you're being chased by red devils. Besides if the Indians should attack the station, Mr Watts will be glad of help.'

Harrington nodded. The stage station was isolated and the Indians might see it as an ideal target.

'We've spent most of the time playing cards,' Mr Turner put in.

'And taking most of my money off me,'

Watts added with a laugh. 'Lieutenant, what do you really think? Are we safe here?'

'About as safe as anywhere. In fact, I'm going back to the fort to report to Captain Maysfield and find out what's happening. I'm not doing any good roaming about out here.'

'Why don't you stay with us tonight and go back tomorrow? There's room for you and the boy so long as you don't mind sharing the floor with Mr Turner and Eddie and listening to them snoring.'

Harrington felt sure he ought to go on, just a bit further towards Wickenburg. Captain Maysfield wouldn't appreciate him taking it easy when there were Indians to be found. But the thought of eating more good food, drinking hot coffee and sleeping, if not in a bed, at least wrapped up in a blanket in front of a fire instead of freezing on the ground with a saddle for a pillow, was too much of a temptation.

Besides he had Timmy to consider. The thought of Rose Watts didn't enter into it.

'Rose, perhaps you can get out more blankets for our visitors?'

'Yes, Pa. Timmy, would you like to help me?'

The little boy stared at her and without saying anything got up to follow her out of the room.

'What will happen to him, Lieutenant?'

'I don't know, Mr Watts. The poor kid is all alone, with no family he knows of. I suppose he'll have to go into an orphanage.'

'Umm, that won't be pleasant for him,' Mr Turner said.

Harrington knew that but what else could he do? He couldn't keep Tim with him, however much he'd like to do so.

'Play some cards, Lieutenant?' Eddie asked.

'I wouldn't,' Watts warned. 'He cheats.'

Harrington smiled. It felt good to be

amongst people who didn't spend all their time waiting for the chance to criticize him. Good to take it easy. It wouldn't last long but he'd make the most of it while he could.

'And you found no trace of either the hostiles or the gunrunners?' Captain Maysfield asked, staring up at the map.

'No, sir.' Ulsen tried not to yawn. He had ridden long and hard to get back to the fort, stopping only for water or when forced to rest his horse. He was tired and dirty, unshaven, his clothes covered in dust.

He'd found the fort no longer sleepy and quiet. Several people from isolated ranches and farms had camped close by for protection. They spent their time either clamouring to know what was being done to capture and kill the Indians or gambling and drinking. They were anxious to return to their homes and Maysfield was just as anxious to see them go.

'I'm pretty sure the Indians ain't on their way to Mexico. Not yet anyway. Not until they've bought the guns and caused some mayhem around here.'

'And that idiot trader the gunrunners stole from thought they were headed towards the mountains?'

'Yes, sir. So did the marshal when I spoke to him.'

'Well I suppose it makes some sort of sense. From San Carlos the hostiles wouldn't have far to travel into the hills and once they buy the guns, they can go anywhere they like while the runners can also make their escape in almost any direction.'

'And escape they'll have to if they're selling faulty guns,' Ulsen added.

'Damn fools! What on earth possessed them? Easy money I suppose,' Maysfield answered his own question. 'And if you're right that's where I've sent Harrington. Damn! He's still wet behind the ears, he'll never manage on his own if he happens to meet up with either party.'

Ulsen didn't think Harrington was quite as incompetent as that but he said nothing. Faced with both hostile Indians and greedy gunrunners anyone, however good, would be in trouble. He didn't want to stop Maysfield sending help after the lieutenant.

'You haven't heard the worst of it,' Maysfield went on, drumming his fingers on the desk.

'Sir?'

'I've had word from Agent Parkin that Black Feather has disappeared too. From what he said he wasn't surprised. Evidently Harrington spoke out of turn and upset the Indian. What's the betting Black Feather has reverted to his old ways and decided to join the bucks on one last raid?'

'Christ. That's all we need.' Red Lance was a hothead, hopefully easily defeated; Black Feather was a planner and an able leader.

'All right, Fred, you go get some rest. I'll see Sergeant Johnson and tomorrow, first thing, you and he can take out a patrol. This time follow Harrington, rescue him from his own foolishness if needs be, and find some hostiles!'

TWELVE

'Did you hear about the time when a skunk got on the stagecoach and wouldn't get off?' Eddie Robertson said. 'All the passengers naturally refused to join it. It didn't look like we were going anywhere.'

'What happened?' Harrington asked. He was sure the stories concerning life on the frontier that Watts and Eddie had been telling weren't true, or were exaggerations, but it didn't matter. They were funny and made everyone, even the rather dour Mr Turner, laugh.

'Oh, in the end the skunk decided he didn't want to go to Sante Fe and he jumped out without paying his fare. But he left a terrible stink behind, ain't that right, Mr Watts?'

'Sure is, Eddie, I remember it well.'

'Oh Pa! Eddie!' Rose protested. 'No more, please!' Realizing that the men wanted to smoke and probably tell other tales not suited to her ears, or Timmy's, she stood and began to gather up the dishes. 'Timmy, come and help me wash up.'

Later when the stories had dried up and the tobacco been put away, Harrington went outside to enjoy some fresh air. It was a calm, warm night, the moon a sliver in the black sky. The smell of sagebrush was strong in the air and from somewhere not too far away came the yipping of a coyote.

Behind him the door opened, letting out the light of a lamp and the noise of people talking, before it was closed again. Harrington knew Rose had come to join him. He half turned to acknowledge her presence and she smiled and came to stand close by, leaning against one of the poles supporting the porch.

He felt awkward. He wasn't used to the

company of young women, the life of an army lieutenant provided few opportunities to meet girls. In Washington he'd enjoyed occasional fumblings with prostitutes but those occasions had been very few and far between and they hardly counted in knowing how to behave with a nice girl like Rose Watts. And she was so pretty, especially now she'd done something with her hair and had on a dress that showed off her figure.

Somewhat nervously he cleared his throat and said, 'It's a lovely night.'

'I love this time of the year.' Rose was almost as awkward as Asa. She usually had no difficulty in making conversation with the stagecoach passengers, but standing out here on her own with a handsome young man was altogether different. He was a lieutenant in the army, responsible for others, with duties that could lead him into danger. What would he think of her, the daughter of a relay station owner who he'd first seen wearing men's trousers?

She forced herself to think of something to say. 'I heard you telling Pa and the others that you were once stationed in Washington. Then you requested to come out here.'

'That's right.'

'Don't you regret leaving Washington with its social whirl?'

Harrington couldn't prevent himself giving an unamused laugh. 'Truly, Miss Watts, as a mere lieutenant with little money and few prospects I was never part of Washington's social scene!'

'But do you like Arizona?'

'It's a harsh country but it does have a certain amount of beauty. What about you?'

'I like its freedom. Sometimes I don't like its cruelty. But there are times when the sun strikes the colours in the rocks or when the spring flowers bloom and I know I couldn't be happy anywhere else.'

'But don't you get lonely?'

'Oh, sometimes. But not often. There's

always something to do and people to meet. I like visiting Wickenburg to shop and gossip with my friends but I wouldn't want to live there. It's too crowded, noisy and smelly. I'm used to being by myself.'

Eddie Robertson nudged Watts as he saw Rose slip out of the door to join Lieutenant Harrington. 'Your little gal is growing up.'

'I know.' Watts didn't know whether to be apprehensive or amused.

His daughter had not only taken the first chance she could to change out of her pants but she had put on not just a divided skirt but a dress—something almost unheard of. She had also tied her hair back into a tidy and becoming bun. She was obviously attracted to Lieutenant Harrington. Watts wasn't worried about leaving her alone with him for he seemed nice enough and Rose ought to be enjoying the attention of young men. At the same time Harrington, like the stagecoach passengers, would come into her life and quickly go out of it again, leaving her alone.

Watts sighed. 'I'll really have to do something for Rosie. She deserves something better than living out here, with just me and a wrangler for company. She should be going to dances and church socials, dressing fashionably and meeting young men.'

'What would you do without her?' Eddie asked.

'That's the trouble. But am I being selfish in keeping her here?'

'Rose might not think so. You should at least discuss the matter with her before making any decisions on her behalf.'

Harrington talked to Rose about army life both on the frontier and in Washington, as well as his growing up in California. He began to think that, given the chance, he could come to like her very much. He hoped she felt the same way about him.

After a while she said, 'It's getting cold. We'd better go in.'

She was right but all the same he was disappointed for he would have liked to stay out here with her for much longer. She smiled at him again as he opened the door and Asa felt his heart skip several beats.

The rest of the evening passed quickly. More cards were played, more stories told. Timmy went to sleep at the table resting against Rose's shoulder.

'We all ought to follow his example,' Watts said, after he'd lost yet another hand to Eddie. 'It's getting late. And perhaps tomorrow we'll get good news and...'

The door crashed open with such force that the wall seemed to shake. Cold night swept into the room.

'What the...!' Harrington exclaimed as everyone looked up, startled and scared.

Rose gave a little cry of fright and moved closer to her father, who put an arm round her.

Timmy came awake with a start.

'Apaches!' he cried.

But it wasn't Indians come to attack them.

Three white men stood in the doorway. One pointed a rifle at them. The second had a gun in one hand, his other arm supporting a younger man, who sagged between his companions. He was bent forward, face creased with pain and he held a red-stained bandage to his side from which blood dripped on to the floor.

THIRTEEN

For a moment everything came to a stop.

Harrington was aware of Watts and Rose together, of Timmy, wide eyed, clinging to Rose's hand. Eddie Robertson stared open mouthed while Mr Turner and Nick Manning went to get up. He should do something. His hand went towards his holstered gun.

The man with the rifle yelled, 'Hold it right there all of you! Don't try anything foolish!'

'That's right.' The other man kicked the door shut behind him and supported his wounded companion further into the room. 'Everyone behaves themselves and they don't get hurt.'

'You're the gunrunners, right?' Harrington said before he could stop himself.

'That's right,' Leroy Sweeney grinned. 'Ain't you the clever one? Don't worry, we ain't out to cause you trouble. All we want is help for my brother. We get that then we leave you good folks to your own business. But in the meantime why don't you take any guns you've got and put them on the floor? Slowly!'

Harrington didn't want to do as the man said but with the two guns pointing at him he, like the others, had no choice.

'That's right. Good. Cliff, pick 'em up.'

'The Indians do that to him?' Watts asked. He left Rose and got up, going towards the men.

Sweeney shook his head. 'It was some goddamn trader over in the hills.'

'Michael Apscott?'

'Yeah, that was his name.'

'Is he dead? Did you shoot him too?'

'No, he ain't dead. Not yet. But we aim to pay him another visit real soon. No more talk, mister, Benny here is badly hurt and I want him made comfortable.'

'And if we don't choose to help you?'

Sweeney raised his gun, pointing the barrel at Watts's face.

'Pa!' Rose cried out.

'You'd just better choose to help, hadn't you? My brother means everything to me and I'm willing to shoot anyone who stops me doing my best for him. Even the boy there. You believe that, mister, and we'll get along fine.'

Harrington knew from the look in the man's eyes that he meant what he said and hoped no one would do anything stupid. 'Watts,' he warned. 'Don't.'

'What do you want?' Watts asked sullenly.

'To get Benny into a bed and his wound seen to. Are you the guy owns this place?'

'Yeah.'

'Then tell me and quick where I can take my brother.'

'My daughter's bedroom is back there.'

Watts nodded at the door that led into the rear of the building. 'That would be best.'

'Is there anyone here knows anything about doctoring?'

Silence.

'Come on! One of you must damn well know something. You live on the frontier, help is miles away, you have to look after yourselves. I'm god-damned waiting!'

'I know a little bit of nursing.' Rose spoke up, going red as the man's attention was turned on her.

'Come with us then.'

'Rose, no.'

'It's OK, old man, I won't hurt her so long as you all remember to behave yourselves. You don't, well, I might not be able to stop myself doing something, we'd all regret. Understand?'

'Yeah, OK.'

'You too, boy,' Sweeney added pointing towards Timmy. 'Come on.'

'Leave him be,' Harrington protested.

'Shut up! The girl and the kid are with me the rest of you won't even think about causing no trouble. Cliff, stay here, keep a watch over these good people. I'm sure they'll know better than to make things difficult.' Sweeney's eyes narrowed as he stared at Harrington. The others looked docile enough, even the relay station owner now he'd been told what was what; this one seemed like he had more fire in him and might cause trouble.

'You, mister, you've got too much to say for yourself, you come with me too where I can keep an eye on you.' It was clear he didn't altogether trust Kendall to handle the situation. 'Anyone tries anything and we both start shooting.'

'Get on over by the table,' Kendall ordered the others. 'Go on, move!'

'Rose, be careful,' Watts said.

'I'll be all right, Pa, don't worry. Come on, Timmy.' She held the boy's hand. 'Don't cry, these men won't hurt us.'

'Help me carry Benny,' Sweeney ordered Harrington.

Asa took hold of Benny round the waist, and Sweeney glared at him as Benny groaned, as if it was his fault. Together the two men carried him through the door, along the short corridor and into Rose's tiny and plain room. It contained only a narrow bed, a table on which an unlit candle stood and a chair. Rose pulled back the bed cover and the two men lay Benny on the bed.

With hands that shook, Rose lit the candle. Harrington wished he could give her some sort of comfort. Tell her it was all right and that these men wouldn't hurt her. But how could he say that when he thought it quite likely that they would hurt them all, for he didn't believe the man's promise to leave them alone?

By the candle's light they could see that Benny's shirt was soaked with blood and he was nearly unconscious.

He looked, to Harrington, as if he was

in a bad way, and that didn't bode well for any of them. As long as they could keep Benny alive they might stand a chance of finding a way out of this. Benny died and his grief-stricken brother was likely to do anything.

'What do you need?' Sweeney asked Rose.

'Water, something to wipe the blood away, and bandages.'

'You, kid, got all that?'

Wordlessly Timmy nodded.

'Then go and fetch what she wants.'

'Let me go,' Rose said. 'He doesn't live here and he won't know where everything is.'

'He can ask one of the others.' Sweeney shoved the boy through the door. 'And be as quick as you can. No tricks or the girl gets shot.'

'There's no need for all your threats,' Harrington said. 'You're the ones in charge, the ones with the guns.'

'Yeah and don't you forget it. Now get

to seeing to Benny and be gentle. Don't hurt him.'

With Rose helping him, Harrington managed to remove Benny's jacket and shirt. The young man moaned in pain several times and each time Sweeney snarled and poked Asa with his gun. Soon Timmy came back carefully carrying a bowl of water, a shirt over his arm.

'Mr Watts said we could use it for a bandage,' he said, putting the bowl down on the table, spilling some of the water.

Sweeney cuffed him about the head for his carelessness and said, 'Tear it into strips then, kid. And hurry it up.'

'Here give it to me.' Harrington took the shirt from Timmy, who had tears in his eyes. 'Go and sit in the corner and be quiet.'

'Yes, sir.'

Harrington tore off one strip of the shirt, handing it to Rose, who began to bathe Benny's wound with it. Soon the bowl of water was red from the blood.

'You be careful, girl, or I'll hurt you too,' Sweeney said as Benny cried out in pain.

'Leave her alone, dammit, she's doing her best. It's not her fault he's been shot.'

'And you, big mouth, shut up.'

Rose turned round from her ministrations. She looked pale. Most of her 'nursing' had been seeing to bumps and bruises, once there had been a broken leg, but she'd never had to cope with a bullet wound before, nor done anything with a gun pointed at her and an unpredictable outlaw with his finger on the trigger. 'The bullet is still in there and I can't take it out.'

'You'll have to.'

'Don't be stupid,' Harrington objected. 'Miss Watts hasn't got the implements or the skill to do something like that.'

'What about you?'

'No, I can't do it. He needs to be gotten to a qualified doctor. There'll be one at

Wickenburg; you should take him there.'

'That'd goddamned suit you, wouldn't it? To get rid of us.'

'Of course it would suit us. But the bullet is deep in his side. He'll surely die if either of us tries to get it out. He needs professional help.'

'I don't like your goddamned attitude!'

'That's too bad. Why don't you accept the truth? Look for yourself'

'Think yourself a big man don't you? Perhaps I should thrash some manners into you.'

'You can try and while you're trying the boy will die.'

Sweeney shoved by Harrington, going over to his brother, staring down at him. He reached out a hand to wipe sweat away from Benny's forehead. He was scared. Benny looked so ill, but he couldn't die, he just couldn't.

'You two stay here, look after him,' Sweeney said to Rose and Timmy. 'See he doesn't hurt none.'

'We'll do our best,' Rose promised.

'You, come with me.' And Sweeney gave Harrington a violent push, sending him sprawling out of the room, and, taking his fear about Benny out on him, kicked him once hard in the ribs. 'Get up! Come on!' And poking him with his gun, he forced Harrington back into the main room.

Kendall had sat down at one end of the table, sprawling along the bench, the rifle within easy reach, while everyone else sat at the other end, tense with worry.

'How's Benny?' Kendall asked, although he didn't particularly care. All he was concerned about was making good their escape.

So he was quite pleased when Sweeney said, 'He's still got the bullet in him. We need to get him to a proper doctor. We'll leave in the morning. We'll take the stagecoach.'

'You can't do that!' Watts protested.

'Sure we can. Who's going to stop us? You?'

'What do we need the stagecoach for?' Kendall asked. 'We've got the buckboard.' Was this another of Leroy's crazy schemes?

'It'll be more comfortable for Benny. And, Cliff, if the army or the Indians are out looking for us, they'll hardly suspect us of riding in the stagecoach. They'll still be looking for the wagon. The old-timer there—' he nodded at Robertson—'can drive it. Hell, he can even take one of the others along to help him if he wants to. But, by God, we're taking it and the rest of you can go to hell.'

No one said anything. They were learning as quickly as Kendall had that once he'd made up his mind it was foolish and pointless to argue with Leroy Sweeney.

'Now, folks, Cliff and me feel like getting some sleep. We've had a hard few days. But I don't exactly trust any of you. So you,' Sweeney nodded at Watts, 'is there anywhere you can be shut up?'

'There's a storeroom with a lock on the door.'

'That'll do.'

'What about Miss Watts and Timmy?' Harrington said. 'You can't lock them up too.'

'I don't intend to, big mouth. They're staying and helping with Benny and don't forget we'll be out here with 'em. So stay put and behave yourselves for the night.'

'Don't worry, we won't do anything.'

'Better damn well not.'

A little later sitting in the dark stuffiness of the small storeroom, listening to the snores of Mr Turner and Eddie Robertson, Watts's feet digging into his back, hardly able to breathe it was so hot, Asa tried to think of a way out; and couldn't.

They were locked in. They had no weapons. He didn't doubt that Leroy Sweeney, at least, would carry out his threat to kill them all, starting with Rose and Timmy. He heard Watts sigh heavily. The man wasn't asleep either. He was too worried about his daughter for that.

What were they going to do?

FOURTEEN

It was morning. Or at least Harrington thought it was. It was too dark in the storeroom for him to tell, for no crack of light came in anywhere. But surely enough time had crawled by for the night to be over.

He felt Watts stir and sit up. 'Lieutenant, you awake?'

'Yes.'

'What's going to happen do you think?'

'I don't know. I hope Sweeney will keep his word and ride away in the stagecoach and leave us behind unhurt.'

'But you don't think he will?'

'Do you? We can describe him and his partners. We know one of them is hurt. He won't want any witnesses left behind to tell all that to the authorities.'

'I wish I knew how Rose was. I'm so worried about her.'

'You've every right to be. But I'm sure she'll be all right all the time Sweeney wants her help with his brother.'

'What are we going to do?'

'We can't just let Sweeney kill us. We can't go down without making some sort of fight of it, although some of us could get hurt.'

'Better that than submitting meekly to the bastards.'

'Are there any other weapons about the place?'

'There's a shotgun we keep in the barn...'

'And there's Mr Turner's gun still on the stagecoach,' Eddie Robertson's voice came out of the darkness. 'I can get that when Nick and me go out to harness up the horses.'

'Anything else?'

'No.'

Oh well, Harrington thought, two guns

were better than none at all. They might just give them the element of surprise over Sweeney and Kendall.

'I wonder how Rose and Timmy are,' Mr Turner said.

'And how the wounded kid is,' Eddie added.

Benny was still alive. Just.

As dawn crept through the shutters into the room Rose woke up. She'd let Timmy have the chair and she was sitting on the floor, her back to the wall.

Carefully, not wanting to wake the little boy, Rose stretched wearily, rubbed her eyes and went over to the bed, holding her breath against what she might find. During the night she'd got up several times to wipe Benny's forehead and to make sure he was comfortable. In the early hours of the morning he had slipped into a deep sleep and she knew she could do no more for him. Now she was relieved to see that he was still breathing, his chest rising and falling shallowly. She lifted his head slightly trying to get him to take a sip of water and behind her she heard the door open.

'How is he?' Sweeney demanded.

'He needs a doctor.'

'All right, all right, I'm damn well goin' to get him one. Get up, you,' he kicked out at the chair Timmy lay in.

'Stop it,' Rose protested. 'He's just a small boy who thanks to you has lost his parents. He can't do you any harm.'

Sweeney shoved his face close to hers. 'Don't try my patience, missy. I want him to get me and Cliff some breakfast. I sure am hungry.'

'I'll have to help him. You can't expect him to do that on his own.'

'All right,' Sweeney said ungraciously. 'Just be quick about it. We wanna be on our way.'

As Rose went out of the bedroom door she almost bumped into Cliff Kendall.

'Oops,' he said and gave her a little half bow.

Rose looked quickly away, feeling scared all over again. She knew most men respected her and would never harm her but she also knew that as a lone woman on the frontier she faced certain perils too.

In the kitchen she said as cheerfully as she could, 'Now, Tim, what do you suggest we cook? Bacon and beans? Coffee, of course. And how about baking some biscuits?'

'Miss Rose, are they going to kill us?' Timmy whispered.

'Of course not.' Rose bent down by him and held him tightly for a moment.

'What are we going to do?'

'I don't think we can do anything except what we're told. You mustn't worry. My pa and Lieutenant Harrington won't let anything happen to us. We must leave things to them and not get in their way.' Leaving Timmy to get things ready, she went into the main room where the two gunrunners had sat themselves down at the table.

'What do you want?' Sweeney growled at her.

'Shall I cook enough for everyone?'

'Yeah, I suppose so.'

'The other men as well?'

'I said yes didn't I?'

'They can't eat locked up.'

'I don't see why not but mebbe I'll let 'em out when the food's ready. And you two behave yourselves in there.'

'Oh, for goodness sake, what do you think we're going to do? I'm a girl and Timmy is a child!'

'I like your spunk,' Kendall called after her.

Sweeney took hold of the key and went over to the storeroom door, unlocking it. 'All right, you can all come out now. Have some breakfast.' He stood to one side of the door, gun in hand, as blinking in the sudden light the men emerged from the room. 'I don't need to remind you who I'll shoot first if any of you tries anything stupid.'

Harrington and Watts looked at one another and Harrington wondered if this was going to be the equivalent of the last breakfast before an execution. The only thing that pleased him was that although Rose and Timmy both looked tired they hadn't been harmed in any way.

'Sit down and eat up,' Kendall called out, good-naturedly, making Harrington long to hit him. 'You ain't got no call to look so worried. We'll soon be on our way and out of your hair.'

'Yeah, and to ensure you continue to behave yourselves, we've decided that we're taking the girl and the kid along with us when we go.'

'You can't!' Watts protested.

Sweeney shoved him down on the bench. 'Sure we can. We've already discussed it with 'em and they're both quite willing. Look, all we're interested in is getting

Benny to a doctor.'

'Yeah and making a profit by selling our furs,' Kendall added, making Sweeney glare at him.

'But we can't have you free to chase us down before Benny is better so we need a couple of hostages to make sure you stay put. Once he's seen a doctor we'll leave 'em at Wickenburg while we get on our way.'

'I refuse to let you take her.'

'You can't stop us. Now shut up you're giving me a headache.'

Watts sat down glancing at Rose. Although she tried to smile reassuringly at him it didn't quite work. He couldn't let her be taken off by these men. Goodness knows what they'd do to her when she was alone with them. And Rose obviously feared the same. He'd never forgive himself if anything happened to her.

Harrington felt much the same way and said, 'Why don't you take me instead?'

'Mister Brave as well as Mister Big

Mouth, ain't you?' Sweeney sneered. 'No, sorry, we take the girl and the kid. Don't worry we'll take real good care of 'em both.'

'Especially the little missy,' Kendall added.

'No!' Harrington said. He half stood up, only to have to sit down again as Sweeney prodded him in the chest with his gun, finger tightening on the trigger. He looked at Watts. They had to do something and time was running out.

'Now while the rest of us eat our breakfast why don't you, old man,' this to Robertson, 'and the idiot boy there go outside and harness up the stagecoach? The sooner you do that the sooner we can leave you alone.'

'Go on, Eddie, Nick,' Watts said.

The meal was eaten in uncomfortable silence. No one, except the two gunrunners, felt much like eating anyway. They were all too worried and scared.

They'd almost finished when Sweeney

suddenly said, 'Hey! Those two are taking their time ain't they? I surely hope they ain't gone off on their own.'

'They wouldn't do that,' Mr Turner said scornfully.

'They are a long while,' Watts admitted suddenly worried. It shouldn't have taken them that long to harness up the stage. Nick might not be clever but he was good with horses. What were they doing? Not something stupid, he hoped. 'Why don't you go and see what they're up to?'

'Oh yeah sure,' Sweeney smiled un-pleasantly. 'What am I? Some kind of fool? No, you, you with the big mouth, you go.' And he pointed his gun at Harrington. 'And don't forget Cliff'll have his rifle pointed at the girl and I'll be standing in the doorway watching you. You try anything he'll shoot her and I won't hesitate to plug you in the back.'

Hoping that Robertson and Nick Manning had managed to get their hands on the two guns and thinking up ways and means of turning the situation to his advantage, Harrington went outside. The morning was already hot, the air still.

He walked slowly over to the corral, rather surprised to see that the horses hadn't yet been hitched to the stagecoach. He hoped that Robertson wasn't considering some kind of stand or ambush from the barn. Harrington badly wanted to go up against Sweeney and Kendall but only when there was a chance of beating them.

'Eddie,' he called. No reply.

He came to a halt and looked back at the house. Sweeney stood in the doorway and he waved his gun at Harrington, ordering him to get on with it.

'Eddie,' he called again.

He rounded the stagecoach. And that was where he found Eddie Robertson and Nick Manning.

They lay on the ground, face down, arrows sticking up in their backs. And flies were already buzzing round their heads where they had both been scalped.

FIFTEEN

'Oh my God!' Harrington exclaimed. In shock, he stumbled backwards, feet getting caught up one with the other so that he almost fell.

The action saved his life.

He heard a whoosh of noise by his ear and an arrow thwacked into the ground where he had been standing.

Further movement caught his eye and he glanced round. He saw a shadowy figure in the barn. The Indians were probably all round him. Yelling, he started to run for the house. He saw Leroy Sweeney staring at him as if he thought Asa was either mad or up to something.

Don't let him shut the door on me, he thought desperately.

He was almost there when an arrow

struck him in the arm. Crying out, he stumbled, but somehow managed to regain his balance and leap for the door. He shoved Sweeney out of the way and threw himself inside, falling to the floor.

'Shut the door!' he yelled. 'Quick!'

For a moment everyone looked at him, unable to take in what was happening. Then they saw the arrow in his arm, the fear in his face—

Indians!

Behind him, Sweeney slammed the door shut and dropped the bar across it. From somewhere in the room Rose screamed once in fright.

Doug Watts began to issue orders. 'Mr Turner, help me bar the windows. Rose, see that the kitchen door is fastened.'

'Are you all right, Lieutenant?' Timmy bent over Asa.

'Lieutenant?' Kendall said, turning from the window where he had opened the loophole so that he could look out. 'You mean, he's a damn soldier boy? Leroy, you hear that? He's a soldier boy. No wonder he was so down on us.'

'Yeah I heard.'

'That hardly matters now, does it?' Watts said angrily. 'In fact you might be glad of a soldier who'll know what to do now the Indians are here.' He turned back to Harrington, who still lay where he had fallen, white-faced with shock. 'Can you stand?'

With his help, Asa climbed to his feet. There was a lot of blood on his shirt sleeve but his arm didn't hurt, in fact it felt numb as if he couldn't raise it. He allowed Watts and an anxious Timmy to help him over to a chair in the corner.

Watts said grimly, 'What about Eddie and Nick?'

Harrington shook his head. 'I'm sorry, they're dead.'

'Oh no!' Rose, who had come back from the kitchen, cried out. 'Oh poor Nick. Poor Eddie.' She put her head in her hands.

'This is no time for tears,' Watts told

her. 'They can come later. Right now I need your help. And so does Tim.' He nodded towards the boy who had gone to stand by Rose's side, fear etched on his face.

Knowing her father was right, Rose gulped back the tears and put an arm round Timmy. 'We'll be all right. We won't let anything happen to you.'

Timmy looked as if he didn't believe her. Hadn't his father said much the same and his father and mother had ended up dead.

'That arrow will have to come out.' Watts said to Asa.

'Then do it. And hurry.'

'Rose, get some water,' Watts said. He helped Asa out of his shirt. 'This is probably going to hurt.' And he got hold of the arrow and tugged. It eased a little, stuck, causing Harrington to moan, and then came free with a little squelchy sound.

'Hurt' was hardly appropriate a word

for the pain that swept over Harrington. Screaming, he sank back on the chair, everything spinning round and threatening to go black. But he couldn't faint. He couldn't. He didn't dare. There was too much to do. Taking several deep breaths, he somehow fought the sick feeling engulfing him, gripping the chair arm with his good hand, until the faintness had gone. Now the arrow was out, his arm had immediately started to ache, like hell.

Carefully Rose bathed the wound, wrapping a bandage round it.

'You're getting good at this,' Harrington said with a little smile he was far from feeling. He wondered if before this was over there would be other patients for her to see to, or whether any of them would even get out of it alive.

'How does it feel?' she asked when she'd finished.

'All right, I think.'

'There's no need to be so brave. You can say if it hurts.' She smiled back at him.

'All right, it hurts.'

Rose smiled again. 'I'm glad you're here. You'll save us, won't you?'

But Harrington didn't know if he could. All his worst nightmares were coming true. He was about to face the hostiles, not with a troop of well-disciplined, well-armed soldiers at his back, charging across open meadows, but here holed up in a house, with ordinary citizens—two men, a girl and a child—and a couple of outlaws for company.

Hell!

He sighed and managed, with Rose's help, to stand up. Somehow preventing himself from moaning, he said, 'Sweeney, I think it would be a good idea if you gave us back our guns...'

Sweeney said a very rude word, indicating what he thought of that idea.

'Don't be a fool. You can't handle the Indians all on your own.'

'He's right,' Mr Turner added. 'For God's sake, man, see sense.

'I ain't that stupid that I'd trust any of you. I still reckon this is some sort of trick that Big Mouth thought up.'

'Oh for Chrissakes,' Harrington said impatiently. 'I had an arrow in my arm! You're an even bigger idiot than I thought.'

'Well, I don't see any Indians.'

At the same moment a high-pitched yelling came from outside and several arrows thunked into the wood of door and shutters. A couple of Indians on horseback dashed towards the house. Timmy ran into Rose's arms, cowering amongst the folds of her skirt.

Kendall shot at the Indians out of the loophole.

'For God's sake, let us defend ourselves!' Watts yelled.

Then the Apaches were by and away and all was quiet again.

'You didn't hit anything!' Sweeney accused Kendall.

'There weren't nothing to aim at. They

were hanging over the side of their animals.'

'Shoot their damn horses then!'

'At least it must prove even to you there are Indians out there, ready to attack us,' Harrington said. 'So, Sweeney, what about those guns?'

'He's right,' Kendall said. 'We might not be able to hold out on our own.'

'Oh all right,' Sweeney reluctantly agreed. 'But any tricks, and I won't wait for the Indians, I'll shoot you myself.'

'OK, OK, we ain't fools,' Watts said. 'We know we need you as much as you need us.'

The Indians swept by again but under fire from several guns, fell back to the barn and the corral.

'They'll be content to stay there, sniping at us,' Harrington said, joining Watts at the window. 'For a while anyway. At least they know we can defend ourselves. What about help coming from Wickenburg?'

'Mebbe. Some time. But they'll have

guessed why the stage has stopped. They won't be worrying about us yet. So there ain't no reason for anyone to come out here. Besides until they hear the Indian trouble is over they won't be any more eager to come here than we are to go into town.' Watts paused. 'What about the soldiers from Fort Fenton? Any chance of them being on the Indians' trail?'

'Captain Maysfield sent me out in one direction, Ulsen, that's the scout, in another. The rest of the soldiers were staying on the fort. I don't think we can rely on the army either.'

'So we're on our own then?'

'Looks like it. What's our position?'

Watts made a quick inventory in his mind. 'We've got plenty of guns and ammunition. I can shoot OK so can you.'

'And I might be short sighted but there's nothing wrong with my aim,' Mr Turner added.

'Perhaps Rose and Timmy can help reload.'

'Rose won't want to do just that. She's as good a shot as me. There's plenty of food and water, enough to last for several days. The walls are pretty stout. And I guess the Indians won't want to spend too much time, or risk getting killed, going up against a well-defended house. We'll be all right so long as we pull together.'

The two men looked at Sweeney and Kendall. They seemed to pose more of a threat than the Indians. But at least Sweeney had given them back their guns and Harrington for one didn't intend to give his up again.

Fred Ulsen came to a halt and took off his hat, wiping the sweat away from his neck. It sure was hot. He reached down for his canteen and took a swig of its warm, brackish water.

Sergeant Johnson came up beside him. 'Anything?'

Ulsen shook his head. 'Nothing since that burnt-out farmhouse last night.'

There someone had buried two bodies, presumably the owner and his wife: had that someone been Asa Harrington? If so, where was he now? Was he still alive? Or had he too been caught by the hostiles and killed? There was, as yet, no sign of anything like that having happened. 'At least we're on the right track. We ought to be on our way.'

'I know you're worried about the lieutenant,' Johnson said, 'but let the men rest here for a while. If anything has happened to Harrington it's happened already and there's nothing rushing around can do to prevent it. The men need a break and so do the horses.'

Ulsen nodded reluctant agreement, knowing that the sergeant was right. If they hurried too much in the desert heat the horses would break down and leave them on foot. And that wouldn't do anyone any good. 'But we'll start off again in an hour. Tell 'em that.'

'Hey!' Kendall suddenly shouted. 'Come here.'

'What is it?' Harrington asked.

'Look! One of the bastards is coming out.'

An Indian on a black horse had ridden into view from the direction of the barn. He was holding something white tied to the end of his lance. He came to a halt some distance away and sat there, straight and tall, looking towards the house.

'It's Black Feather!' Sweeney said.

'Black Feather?' Harrington said in surprise. 'It can't be. I saw him at the Reservation.'

'Well it is. The sonofabitch is here. What the hell does he want?'

'He's after a pow-wow by the looks of things,' said Watts. 'That's meant to be a white flag of truce he's carrying. Don't you agree, Lieutenant?'

'OK, so he wants to talk to us. Supposing we don't want to talk to him?' Sweeney raised his gun.

Quickly Harrington knocked it down. 'Don't shoot! Don't be stupid!'

'What the...' Sweeney turned on him angrily.

'Don't you see, this could be our chance to get out of this.'

'Fat chance,' Kendall muttered.

'We should at least hear what he has to say.'

'All right, Lieutenant, then who the hell is going out there? Not me, for certain.'

'Well someone has got to go and quick,' said Watts. 'Or he'll get fed up and change his mind.'

'You, soldier boy,' Sweeney said shoving at Harrington, while Kendall looked on and grinned. 'You know it all and you've always got so much to say for yourself, you go out there and talk to Black Feather.' And he stepped back, opened the door and pointed his gun at Harrington. 'Go on! Or I'll shoot you myself!'

SIXTEEN

The door was shut behind Harrington. He grimaced nervously. Black Feather probably wouldn't be very pleased to see him—it was quite likely his rudeness to the Indian at the Reservation was the reason why he was here. And he, not knowing what to say, certainly didn't want to speak to Black Feather.

Still, there was nothing else for it. Sweeney wouldn't let him back in the house and the Indian still sat on his horse, waiting.

Wishing his heart wouldn't pound quite so hard nor his mouth feel so dry, Harrington stood up straight, held his arms out from his sides, so that Black Feather would know he wasn't about to reach for his gun, and walked slowly and carefully towards the man.

'Leroy, Leroy, what's happening? Where am I?' The voice sounded weakly from the direction of Rose's bedroom. 'Leroy!'

'That's Benny, he's awake.' Relief lit up Sweeney's face. 'I must go and see him. Cliff, you keep an eye on these here good people.'

As Leroy hurried away, Kendall pointed his gun at Watts and Mr Turner. 'I don't want to shoot you.'

'Well, I'd quite like to shoot you,' Watts muttered.

'Old man, you're getting on my nerves. Don't make me do something we'd all regret.'

Benny had raised himself up on the pillows and he stared with frightened, pain-filled eyes as Sweeney came into the room.

Leroy went over to his brother, reaching out a hand to feel his forehead to find that, thank God, the fever had almost gone. He held Benny's hand. 'How do you feel?'

'I ain't sure. I hurt. Where are we?'

'At the Watts' stagecoach relay station. Do you remember anything about it?'

Benny shook his head. 'The last thing I remember is being bounced around in the wagon. Who bandaged me up?'

'The daughter of the station owner. A real nice young lady if you get my drift. Cliff has got his eye on her for sure.'

'Am I goin' to die?'

''Course you ain't.' But Sweeney gave a nervous laugh and went on reluctantly. 'Benny, I'm afraid the bullet is still in your side.'

Benny went even whiter and looked more scared than before. 'Leroy, tell me the truth, I am goin' to die, ain't I? I sure hurt enough. I don't wanna die. You gotta help me. Get me to a doctor.'

'That's what we were trying to do. Unluckily we've landed in a spot of bother.'

'What do you mean?'

'The Apaches, led by Black Feather, are outside.'

'Oh, God, no,' Benny moaned in despair. 'We're all dead for sure.'

'No we ain't. I won't let that happen.'

Benny didn't feel well enough to point out that Leroy had rarely been able to stop anything bad happening in the past. Instead he groaned and said, 'I could do with something to drink. My mouth is real parched.'

'All right. But it'll have to be water, I don't think the good folks here have got any whiskey.' Benny pulled a face. 'I'll get the little lady to bring it in for you, seeing her pretty face will cheer you up.'

'Yeah, OK.'

At that moment Kendall sauntered in, leading a sullen Timmy by the arm.

'Hey,' Sweeney objected, 'why have you left the others alone?'

'I told 'em I'd shoot the kid if they tried anything. I just came to see how Benny was.' Actually Kendall had been hoping to hear that Benny was near to death and he was sorry to see the young man sitting up in bed, looking as mean as ever.

'I'm real hurt.'

'You don't look so bad to me.'

'Well he is.'

'Why don't we move the bed over to the window and prop him up?'

'Why do you want to do that, Cliff?'

Kendall ignored Sweeney's ominous tone and said, 'So Benny can keep watch at this side of the house and shoot any of the bastards if they put in an appearance.'

'I can't,' Benny wailed. 'I'm too hurt.'

'There's no way he can do anything like that,' Sweeney said angrily. 'He's wounded and in pain. Don't be a fool.'

'Then why don't the kid stay in here with him? He can watch out for the Indians and Benny can watch out for the kid.'

'I don't want to. I want to stay with Miss Rose,' Timmy cried, near to tears, trying to pull away.

'Be quiet.' Kendall hit him round the side of his head.

'Good idea. We'll do that. Help me push the bed against the wall then go back to the others.'

'Leroy.' Benny called his brother back just as he was going out of the door. 'I see Cliff is still here causing trouble as usual.' He fingered the quilt, looking down at it. 'I just wondered whether he might, before all this is over, be, well, you know, killed by the Indians.'

Sweeney looked at him suspiciously, wondering what he meant.

'Be more for us. And we'd never get the blame.'

Sweeney smiled, realizing exactly what his younger brother was suggesting. He went outside to the main room, where the others waited anxiously. 'What's going on?'

Mr Turner turned from the window. 'The lieutenant is having quite a parley with your friend. Everything else is quiet.'

Harrington saw Black Feather's eyes narrow angrily as he recognized him. Behind him another younger Indian came out of the barn. Black Feather slid off his horse, handing the reins to Red Lance and stood, arms crossed against his chest, waiting for Harrington to reach him.

'Black Feather,' Harrington acknowledged. 'I'm surprised to find you here. After your concerns of the other day, I thought you had decided it was foolish to go on the warpath.'

'Sometimes, considering the attitudes of those in charge of us and our welfare, there seems little left to do to let people know how we feel and what we are suffering, but to go on the warpath, however foolish it might turn out.'

'I'm sorry for what happened.'

'It's too late for that.'

'This could still be worked out.'

'Sure, and we'd be locked up in jail,' Red Lance spoke up angrily. 'Hanged too probably.'

'The people in the house are innocent of doing you harm. You can have no quarrel with them. They're far from the Reservation.'

Black Feather's eyes sparked angrily. 'It's not them we're interested in.'

With a sinking feeling, Harrington suddenly realized that the Indians must have followed the gunrunners here and knew very well they were sheltering inside. Although why that should anger the Indians so much he couldn't guess.

'Then why are you here?'

'Just because I am a red man, don't think you can insult my intelligence, Lieutenant. The three white men sold us useless guns.'

So that was the reason; Harrington's heart sank even further. My God, what a stupid thing to do.

'Did you know that? They do not fire, the ammunition doesn't work. If we had used them in a raid we would have been killed. Oh, I realize that would probably have suited your purpose...

161

'I don't want to see anyone hurt.'

'...but it would hardly have suited mine. One of Red Lance's friends has already been badly hurt when a gun exploded in his face.'

'I suppose that's why you killed the two white men here with arrows?' Harrington spoke as bitterly as Black Feather. 'One of whom was probably no older than Red Lance's friend. I'm sorry about him, but I'm just as sorry for the men you've killed and scalped.'

'That was before I arrived. It was a mistake. I wouldn't have let it happen.'

'Well it's a shame you were cheated. But it seems that was a chance you took dealing with traitors. You shouldn't have trusted them. Now, what is it you want?' Harrington had a feeling he knew very well what Black Feather wanted and the Indian's next words confirmed his worst fears.

'We want the three white men handed over to us.'

'I can't do that.'

'I would then guarantee that the rest of you, even you, Lieutenant, would be left alone and unharmed.'

'I still can't agree to it.'

'Why not?' The demand was made angrily. 'You said yourself these men are traitors. They are the ones responsible for most of the trouble that has been caused. Red Lance and his friends would never have left San Carlos had they not learned about the guns. It has not mattered to those three white men that other white men and women have already been killed or that more may die. It certainly has not mattered to them that Indians too will die. All they have been concerned about is furs and money. What, Lieutenant, do you owe them?'

'They're white...'

'And I'm red.' Black Feather spoke bitterly. 'And that is all that matters, is it not, Lieutenant?'

'Of course it's not. But I can't hand

163

white men over to you to be tortured and killed.'

'What do you intend to do with them?'

'Take them back to Fort Fenton where they will stand trial.'

'And where they will probably be found not guilty. I know quite a lot about white man's justice.'

Harrington shook his head. 'I don't think that will happen.'

'Don't you?'

'No. But even if it does I have no choice but to protect those men from you. I'm sorry but that's the way it is.'

'Then I am sorry too. My quarrel is with those three men and I would have been willing to let the rest of you go free. But as you will not agree to that and as they're under your protection then I have no choice but to order the attack. It probably means none of you will leave here alive!'

SEVENTEEN

'I don't see why we can't hand 'em over to the Indians,' Mr Turner stated. 'They're nothing to us. I say they deserve whatever comes to 'em.'

Sweeney turned angry eyes on the guard. 'If it weren't that we might need you I'd shoot you down right here. And iffen you say another goddamn word I will anyway.'

'It's all right,' Kendall said. 'The soldier boy there wouldn't hand us over even if he could, which he can't, ain't that so?'

Harrington nodded. 'It wouldn't be right.'

Mr Turner risked more displeasure. 'I don't see why not.'

'They'd be tortured and...'

'So what? They're traitors! Willing for

white people to get killed as well as Indians. And by handing 'em over we'd be left in peace.'

'You believe an Apache?' Sweeney sneered.

'As much as I believe you.'

The two men squared up one to the other and Harrington stepped between them, pushing them apart. The last thing he wanted was for them to start squabbling amongst themselves. And while it would solve several problems if Sweeney was shot in a gunfight it wouldn't help if the same thing happened to Mr Turner. 'Stop it the pair of you.'

'It's all very well pleading duty and what's right and what's wrong,' Doug Watts said. 'But, Lieutenant, you might remember there's my daughter and a small boy to consider. What will happen to them?'

Harrington sighed. Sometimes it was difficult to remember where duty lay, especially when he didn't want to carry it out, and when it meant siding with the likes of Leroy Sweeney.

Rose came to his rescue. 'Pa, you can't expect Asa...Lieutenant Harrington...to do what Black Feather wants. You wouldn't even be suggesting he should if it wasn't for me. And I wouldn't want something like that on my conscience.'

'Nice of you to say so,' Kendall leered, making Rose regret what she'd said.

'Look!' Sweeney yelled, making them all jump. 'Look! It ain't nothing to do with any of you, not even the big-mouth soldier boy. I'm the one in charge here. And I'm saying that me and Cliff and Benny ain't goin' out there! And that's final! I don't wanna hear another goddamned word about it! The next one who says any different I'll shoot down. Understand?'

'You forget,' Mr Turner said, 'you ain't necessarily in charge now we've got our guns back.'

'You ain't likely to use 'em on us.'

'You don't know that.'

'For Chrissakes!' Kendall shouted. 'Can't all of you see it'd be best if we stopped arguing and pulled together? Or we could all end up being tortured by the damn Apaches.'

The argument that had raged since Harrington returned from his parley with Black Feather suddenly ceased as Watts shouted, 'Oh God, here they come again!'

'Rose! Come with me!' Harrington ran out of the room and into the kitchen, drawing his gun as he did so.

Rose paused on the way to look in on Timmy, who crouched by the window, while Benny sat up in bed, holding a rifle across his lap. Timmy turned a pale face towards her.

'Don't worry, Tim, they won't hurt you.'

'No, but I will if he doesn't stop whining,' Benny said nastily.

'How could you?' Rose snapped. 'Oh that bastard!' she said as she joined Harrington, who was firing out of the kitchen window. 'I wish I'd shot him myself!' She took a deep breath to calm down. 'What do you want me to do?'

'Stand by the window, I'm going by the door.' But before Harrington could get there, they heard a thump from above.

'Someone's on the roof!' Rose cried.

'Can I get up there from inside?'

'Yes. There's a trapdoor just outside my bedroom. Be careful.'

'I will.'

Sticking his gun in his belt, Asa went into the corridor. He could hear steady firing coming from the parlour and the odd shot from Benny. He saw the trapdoor and reached up pushing it open. Grabbing its edge, he hefted himself up through the opening.

It seemed that the Indian having got on the roof had then not known what to do. He was leaning against the low wall surrounding the roof and peering over the edge. But as Harrington scrambled up he swung round. Screaming in excitement he rushed towards him, bundling into him before Asa had got his footing. The two young men tumbled to the ground and Harrington just managed to grab the Apache's knife hand before the blade was plunged into his chest.

He punched the Indian hard in the side and the Indian caught hold of his hair, tugging it so hard tears came into his eyes. Somehow Harrington got his legs under him and kicked up sending the Apache flying off of him.

The Indian was up before Harrington, slashing out with his knife. It slit Asa's sleeve but didn't cut him. Harrington dodged out of the way and as the Indian came at him again he shoved him away. The Apache missed his footing, stumbled against the wall and fell. Before he disappeared, Harrington saw the panic in his face and made a grab for him but the Indian had pitched over the side before he could get there. This time the young man's scream was one of terror; a cry abruptly cut off as he hit the ground.

Breathing heavily, Harrington rested for a moment his hands on his knees. The wound in his arm was bleeding, he could feel the sticky wetness trickling down to his wrist, otherwise he was unhurt. And the shooting had stopped.

'Lieutenant? Asa?'

He straightened and a bit shakily went over to the trapdoor seeing Rose staring anxiously up at him. 'It's all right.' He climbed through the trapdoor, pulling it shut behind him. It bolted on the inside and he slid the bolt closed, hoping it would hold.

'You're hurt,' she cried, seeing the blood.

'It's just from the arrow wound in my arm. I must have wrenched it.'

'I'll see to it.'

'In a minute. Let's find out if everyone is OK first.'

'I got one of the bastards!' Benny was shouting from the bedroom. 'Shot the sonofabitch right off his horse!'

'A couple of the others were wounded too,' Watts added. 'And you killed one, Lieutenant. I doubt they'll make a full out attack like that again. We hit 'em too hard.'

'No one here is hurt?'

'No, Lieutenant. I told you this old place has stout walls.'

'What now?' Sweeney turned from the window, face alight with the thrill of the fight.

'I agree with Mr Watts. They won't risk another attack like that. But—' Harrington was trying to remember all he'd been taught at West Point about Apaches and the way they fought—'it doesn't mean we can afford to relax. In fact, it might be worse for us.'

'Do you mean something by that or are you just trying to frighten us?' Sweeney demanded.

'I mean that not only will they wait us out but they'll try to sneak up on us.

So we continue to watch the doors and the windows. Or we might find that the next time we look out an Apache will be looking in.'

'We'll handle 'em,' Sweeney boasted.

Harrington and Watts were right. The Indians contented themselves with appearing now and then to shout taunts at the besieged, or occasionally firing at the house. They had no hope of hitting anything; their plan was to keep everyone inside anxious and upset.

'The worst of it is we can't do anything,' Watts said. 'I suppose us attacking them is out of the question?'

'It'd be difficult but it might be worth trying if it wasn't for Rose and Timmy. We daren't do anything to risk their lives. Anyway Sweeney and Kendall would never agree. They know they're safe inside. And the situation is different to what we thought at first.'

'What do you mean?'

'This isn't just a random attack by the Apaches, it's planned. They won't just give up and go away, they're going to do all they can to kill us all.'

'Hey, you two, stop plotting!' Sweeney yelled as he came back into the room from seeing how Benny was. 'You, girl, my brother wants some water, get it for him.'

Rose cast an anxious look at Harrington as she went by him. She'd told him Benny was still conscious but he was white-faced with pain and, despite her best efforts, after his exertions of firing out of the window his wound had started to bleed again.

Slowly the day dragged on. It was hot and stuffy and dark in the house with all the windows and doors shut. And, despite the danger, boring too with nothing to do, except keep watch and stay out of each other's way.

Being pinned down as they were soon got on everyone's nerves. Harrington knew it would be bad enough if two of their number weren't violent and unpredictable outlaws. As it was he was scared trouble would break out any minute from those inside the house let alone from those without.

He began almost to wish the Indians would attack so something would happen!

EIGHTEEN

As the sky darkened outside, Sweeney wiped sweat away from his forehead and turned to where Watts and Rose sat together at the table. 'Hey, you girl, go and get us something to eat.'

'Yeah, Rosie, good idea,' Watts agreed. 'I'll help you.'

'No, you won't.' Sweeney waved the rifle at him. 'Just the girl. You stay here where I can keep an eye on you.'

'Don't worry, Pa, I'll manage.'

As Rose left the room Kendall sidled up to Sweeney. 'Leroy, I'm worried.'

'What about? The Indians? We're safe enough.'

'No, not the Apaches,' Kendall interrupted. 'About what might happen afterwards.'

'What d'you mean?'

'Seems to me we're stuck like rats in a trap. We can't leave because of the Indians outside yet to stay is asking for trouble too.'

'The Indians ain't goin' away, we've gotta stay.' Sweeney looked at his partner as if he didn't know what he was talking about.

'Yeah and the only way we'll get out of here is if either the army or someone from Wickenburg comes to rescue us.'

'Yeah? So?'

'So, Leroy, if that happens then these good people will hand us over to 'em. Can you see the soldier boy, Watts or Mr Turner pretending they don't know why the Indians attacked the station or that they don't know who we are? No, they'll say, look, here are the gunrunners responsible for all this trouble, and we'll be led away in chains.'

Although it was his future, or lack of it, at stake, Kendall couldn't prevent himself gloating a little. Yet another of Sweeney's schemes had gone disastrously wrong because he wouldn't listen to anyone except himself.

'With Benny not up to doing anything, there are more of them than there are of us, and now they've got their guns back.' Kendall raised his hands as Sweeney scowled angrily. 'I know you didn't have no choice 'bout that but can you see any of 'em hesitating to shoot us?'

'We'll just have to shoot them first.'

'That might not be so easy if our rescuers are piling in through the door.'

'I'll have to think on it,' Sweeney muttered. He wasn't worried about himself, nor about Kendall—the bastard was enjoying this—but no way was he going to let anything more happen to Benny.

'I wouldn't be surprised if those sonsofbitches weren't planning something right now to try and overpower us. I reckon the only way to stop 'em is if we keep the girl and the kid close by us.' Kendall got a faraway look in his eyes. 'The girl especially. She sure is nice looking and it sure is a long while since I had me a willing woman.'

'I don't think this one would be willing.'

'She would be, eventually. That's why you sent her out to the kitchen on her own so I could be with her, ain't it?'

It hadn't been, Sweeney had been thinking of his stomach, but now he smiled and patted his friend on the shoulder. If Kendall had his way with the girl it would keep him quiet and on Sweeney's side, which Leroy wanted for the time being at least.

Kendall returned the smile. 'I'll see you later.' He was aware of both Harrington and Watts watching him as he went out; he didn't take any notice of either of them.

As she heard the door open, Rose glanced up from peeling potatoes. She hoped it was Asa but her heart sank as she saw Cliff Kendall. What did he want? Well, he certainly didn't want to help her with the cooking! She kept a firm grip on the knife.

'Hello there, Miss Watts, need me to do anything?'

'No.' Rose hoped her voice didn't betray her fears.

'Nothing at all?'

'No. Why don't you leave me alone? I don't want anything to do with you.'

'I suppose you think I ain't good enough?' Kendall said sulkily. 'I bet you'd be willing if I was the soldier boy.'

'Maybe. But you're not him, are you?' Rose turned back to the table.

'I'll show you I'm better than him.' And Kendall stepped close, put his arms round her waist and nuzzled her neck with his lips.

'Oh!' Rose exclaimed, both angry and scared. 'How dare you!'

Kendall swung her round and, gripping her arms tightly, kissed her. Rose struggled furiously, and Kendall was so concerned with holding her still and trying to kiss her at the same time that he didn't hear someone come in behind him.

'Let her go!' Harrington roared. He grabbed Kendall by the shoulder and pulled him away from Rose who collapsed back against the table. 'You bastard!' And he hit the man hard round the jaw.

Kendall stumbled backwards, fumbling for his gun. Harrington kicked out at the man's hand and with a cry Kendall dropped the revolver. Quickly the two men set to fighting, punching and kicking, falling to the floor. Harrington was so furious he wanted to kill the man for what he'd tried to do, *would* kill him...

'Get off him!' Sweeney yelled and caught hold of a handful of Asa's hair, pulling him up by it. He shoved him away then turned to help Kendall to his feet.

Scared the two men might hurt both him and Rose, Harrington's hand snaked down to draw his gun. He was aware of Rose, knife still in her hand, by the table and then Watts and Mr Turner appeared in the doorway. Was this the time to overcome the two gunrunners? But before Asa could get his gun out of its holster, Sweeney was ready for them all, he had the rifle in his hand, was passing Kendall his revolver.

The moment was lost before it began as Sweeney stuck the rifle barrel against Harrington's chest. 'Don't try anything.'

'You stay away from my daughter or I'll make you sorry you were ever born.'

'I'm not hurt,' Rose said quickly, not wanting her father to do anything silly.

'You bastard,' Harrington said to Kendall. 'I was just trying to be friendly. I didn't mean no harm.'

'Get out of here, both of you. Go on. Mr Turner go with 'em,' Watts ordered. Once they'd gone he went over to his daughter. 'Are you sure you're all right, Rosie?'

'Yes, Pa.' She clung to him for a moment. 'Thanks to Lieutenant Harrington.' She smiled at him over her father's shoulder.

'I knew the bastard was up to something.' Harrington was still furious; and frustrated because he hadn't had the chance to beat Kendall up.

'I'll finish dinner.' Rose pulled away from Watts.

'Do you want me to stay with you?'

'No, Pa, I'll be OK, really.' Rose wanted to be alone; to cry for a while, to give thanks for her escape; mostly to think about Asa Harrington.

'Come on,' Harrington said to Watts. 'I won't let anything happen to you, Rose.'

'I know.' And she smiled again.

Harrington stopped Watts in the corridor outside the parlour door. 'We've got to do something. The longer we're here like this, the worse it's going to get. Sweeney and Kendall are both dangerous, they're also impatient and scared, a bad combination. And the next time we might not be able to stop Kendall from hurting Rose.'

Watts bit his lip. 'That's what I'm scared of.'

'And they're not the only danger. What happens if the Indians do overpower us?'

'What can we do? Draw down on those two?'

'I wish we could but it's too risky. They're watching us the same as we're watching them.'

'What then?'

'I've been thinking about it. One of us should go and get help.'

'That would be risky too.'

'But only for one of us.'

'Who?'

Harrington sighed. 'It'll have to be me. Mr Turner is too old, you've got Rose to think of, Sweeney and Kendall wouldn't do it.'

That left him. He didn't want to go out there, alone, amongst hostile Indians who hated him as one of their enemies—a soldier—but he could see no alternative.

Nor could Watts. 'You'll have to get a horse. It won't be easy with the Indians in the barn but to go on foot to Wickenburg will take you too long. What about weapons?'

'I'll take my revolver. You're more likely to need the rifle. And if I have to use a gun it means I haven't gotten away and it probably won't do me any good anyway.'

'When will you go?'

'I don't see any reason to delay. I'll go tonight.'

NINETEEN

'I dunno 'bout this,' Sweeney objected when told about Harrington's plan.

'We've got to do something,' Harrington said with an impatient sigh. 'We can't hold out forever. Don't forget it's not just any Indian out there, it's Black Feather. On his own Red Lance would probably get bored and give up but Black Feather is wily and clever. How many sieges like this do you think he's been involved in? He's probably plotting right now how to get in here. And the fact that he's left a trail of dead white men in his wake while he's still alive shows he knows what he's doing.'

'The soldier boy is right,' Kendall put in.

'Why should he be the one to go?'

'Do you want to?'

'Are you sure you ain't got cold feet and have decided to run out on us?'

Harrington went red with anger at this slur. 'Don't tar me with the same brush as yourself.'

'I ain't a coward.'

'No, just a thief and a traitor.'

'There's your brother to think of as well,' Watts put in in an attempt to stop the argument between Harrington and Sweeney before it got any worse. He was quite sure that if they remained in the same room for much longer, Sweeney would draw his gun and start shooting; the only thing stopping Harrington from doing the same was the thought that someone besides Leroy might get hurt. 'Benny needs help. The longer he goes without proper doctoring the worse he'll be.'

All the anger and fight went out of Sweeney. Benny was awake again, moaning and feverish. And these good people didn't even have any whiskey to give him to stop the pain. 'All right,' he agreed and added, having to have the last word, 'But you'd better not be doing anything other than bringing help back here.'

'Supper's ready,' Rose said coming into the room with the plates. Timmy was by her side, helping her. 'Tim, go and sit by Lieutenant Harrington. Oh! What's that?'

From outside came the sound of a monotonous drumbeat, followed soon after by a loud chant.

'Black Feather is telling us he's still out there,' Watts said.

Sweeney went over to one of the windows, peering out of the loophole. From the direction of the barn came the glow of a fire but otherwise there was nothing to see. 'How long is that goddamned noise goin' to go on for?' he demanded.

'They'll keep it up all night I reckon,' Watts said. 'In an effort to stop us getting any sleep. Don't worry, it don't mean anything. Come and eat now Rose has cooked this for you.'

'Talking of tonight,' Harrington said, helping himself to potatoes, 'one or two of you had better stay awake and keep guard.'

'Yeah, don't worry, we'll take it in turns. That is if any of us gets any sleep with that racket going on.'

Watts turned to Harrington. 'It might help you. The more Indians involved with the singing and dancing the less there'll be watching this place.'

Harrington nodded. It was what he hoped as well. Timmy gave a muffled sob and realizing the boy was upset—he'd already lost his parents, now it must look as if he was in danger of losing the man who had rescued him—Asa reached over to ruffle his hair. 'I'll be as quick as I can, Tim, I promise. And while I'm gone will you be a good boy and look after Miss Rose for me?'

'Yes, sir,' Timmy mumbled, staring down at his plate so that no one saw the tears in his eyes.

'Oh, Asa, I wish you weren't going,' Rose said later on that evening.

'Believe me, I don't want to go out there on my own. I don't want to leave you. But I've got to. We need help.'

'You will be careful won't you?'

'Of course I will.'

'And you will come back?'

'Yes.' Harrington put his arms round her pulling her close to him. She raised her face to his and his lips found hers. For a long moment they clung together, kissing, but although he wanted to hold on to her forever he quickly pushed her away. She was crying. 'Rose, make sure nothing happens to Tim for me?'

'Yes.'

'Take Tim and stay in your room with Benny tonight. Sweeney won't let Kendall bother you there.'

'All right. I'm not scared.' Rose spoke bravely but she fooled neither herself nor Harrington.

Asa kissed her again and she followed

him as he went into the dark kitchen where Watts waited for him. There was nothing left to say that hadn't already been said and Asa simply shook the man's hand. He opened the door and, taking what might be a last look at Rose, slipped through it. The door was shut and barred behind him. He was alone in the night.

Keeping close to the side of the house, Asa stayed where he was until his eyes became used to the dark. The sound of the drumming was much louder out here and although he listened hard he couldn't hear anything above it. An Indian might be close by and he wouldn't know, but perhaps that also meant the chanting Indians wouldn't hear him either.

Pulling his gun from its holster Asa moved forward. He reached the end of the house where an open space stretched before him in all directions. He stared towards the corral and the horses. Unfortunately that was where the Indians were dancing and singing.

But he must have a horse.

Taking a deep breath he bent double and crept towards the corral.

While all round him the soldiers snored and grunted, Fred Ulsen couldn't sleep. He was too worried. That afternoon they had crossed the path of the Indians. They were moving in the direction of Wickenburg. He didn't know why they should be going there—Wickenburg was surely too large for the Indians to attack. Red Lance might want to make his name by doing so but Black Feather would counsel against such a foolish decision. And then they had seen the tracks of a horse and buckboard being driven hard.

'The gunrunners?' Sergeant Johnson speculated.

'I imagine so,' Ulsen agreed.

And he had suddenly known what the Indians were doing in the area. They were after the gunrunners who had cheated them by selling them useless guns.

He was determined to be on the way at first light.

Harrington was almost at the corral when he heard a noise off in the brush to his left. He came to an abrupt halt and strained his eyes in that direction. At first he couldn't see anything but then he made out the slight shape of an Indian huddled down in the bushes. The Apache must have been so intent on watching the house that he hadn't seen Harrington, although he had passed quite close by.

Asa didn't know what to do. If he moved again the Indian must notice him; yet he couldn't stay where he was because if the Indian happened to glance in his direction he would see him anyway. He couldn't use his gun. A shot would alert the Apaches whooping it up by the barn; so would a hand to hand fight.

Suddenly the Indian gave a sharp intake of breath. It had been taken out of Harrington's hands. The Indian had spotted him! He acted quickly, instinctively. Before the Indian could get to his feet he rushed over to him, raised his gunhand and brought the gunbutt down hard on the Indian's head. With a little sigh the Apache collapsed back to the ground.

Harrington stood up, breathing hard. He was drenched with sweat, his shirt clammy, sticking to his back. But obviously no one else had seen or heard anything for the drumming and chanting was going on without pause. Waiting a moment or two to let his heart cease racing, he went over to the corral, crouching by the wall. The horses were nearby and they were quiet so that he didn't think any of the Apaches was guarding them.

He slipped over the wall, holstered his gun and holding out his hand went over to his horse. The animal gave a whicker of recognition and came up, nuzzling him. He stroked its nose several times. He daren't wait to saddle or bridle it; he'd have to ride it bareback. He grabbed a handful of the horse's mane and clambered up on to its back. It gave a squeal of surprise at being treated in such a way and did a little sideways dance before settling down.

Harrington kicked it into a walk with his heels.

'Hey!' The shout came from over by the barn. The drumming and singing stopped abruptly.

Harrington didn't understand the shouts that followed. He didn't need to. Because he understood only too well that he'd been seen!

'Come on!' he yelled and kicked the horse again, much harder this time. It gave another snort and leapt into the air, darting into a gallop. The corral wall appeared in front of it and Harrington felt the horse get ready to take the jump. He clung to its mane and pressed his knees into its sides, praying that he wouldn't fall off.

TWENTY

The horse sailed over the corral wall, stumbling as it landed. Harrington's heart lurched and he clutched the animal's mane even tighter in the effort to stay on. The horse righted itself and took off at a gallop. Asa risked a look behind him. The Indians milled around, pointing after him, waving their arms. Then several of them raced into the corral catching up the other horses. They were coming after him!

Harrington urged the horse to go faster. He could hear the Apaches whooping and yelling, there were several shots, followed by the pounding of hooves. He glanced back again. His hand strayed towards his revolver but he quickly gave up on that idea. No way could he draw the gun, turn and shoot and stay on the horse. And it was doubtful he would hit anything. Better to concentrate on getting away.

With the first shots Rose sat up from her uncomfortable position on the floor. A hand strayed to her mouth. Asa had been seen, the Indians were shooting at him! She got up and went outside to the kitchen where her father stood by the window, trying to see what was happening.

'Pa?'

Watts turned to look at his daughter. 'I can't make anything out.'

'Have they caught him?'

'I don't think so. They're still firing; listen.' The sound of the shots was getting fainter. 'I reckon the lieutenant got a horse and some of the Indians are chasing after him.'

'Oh God,' Rose whispered. 'Oh, please let him be all right.'

Watts took hold of her in his arms. 'I know it ain't easy but there's nothing we can do, except wait. How's the boy?'

197

'Timmy is fast asleep, he didn't wake up.'

'That's good. And, Rosie, you should try and get some sleep yourself.'

'How can I sleep?'

'Staying awake and worrying won't do anyone any good, not even the lieutenant. And you might need to be wide awake to deal with tomorrow.'

'Why? What do you mean?'

'If the lieutenant gets away, and pray God he does, the Indians will know he's gone for help. They'll want to get whatever they've in mind over and done with quickly.'

'They'll attack us again?'

'Yeah, and this time they may not give up so easily.'

Harrington knew he couldn't escape if he kept to the desert floor. It was too flat, too easy for the Indians to keep him in sight. And they would want to stop him from getting help. The hills were too far away, he could be caught before he reached them, but nearby was the creek...

Pulling on the horse's mane he turned the animal in the direction of the trees, losing several precious moments as he did so. An Apache appeared close by and Asa banged his horse into the smaller Indian pony and kicked out at the other man as he passed by. The Indian tumbled off his pony's back and although he quickly got to his feet and loosed off an arrow it came nowhere near.

They entered the trees, the low branches whipping at Asa as the horse hardly slowed. The creek came up at them fast. There was a steep bank, some rocks and then the water, deep and fast flowing, even at this time of the year.

'Come on, boy, don't let me down now,' he urged the horse and sent it flying down the bank. Above him he heard the Indians—they'd caught up!

Halfway down the slope the horse slipped and went down on its front legs.

Harrington's grip on its mane loosened and he sailed over the animal's head, landing with a jolt. Yelling with fright and pain he bounced once then started to roll down the steep slope, gathering speed as he went.

Every bump hurt, rocks tore at his skin and clothes, he couldn't stop himself. His horse hit the creek first, sending up a cascade of water. It whinnied with fright but, unhurt, it scrambled up the far bank, galloping away.

The rocks at the foot of the bank came up to meet Harrington fast and he crashed into them. For a moment he lay there, catching his breath, wondering if anything was broken. Everything hurt too much for him to be able to tell. He wanted to give up and stay there but quickly changed his mind when an arrow skimmed off the rock nearest to him and several shots were sent in his direction. He looked up. The Indians were starting down the slope after him.

Groaning and wincing, he clambered to his feet and bending low ran across the rocks. He half dived, half fell into the water, going under, the water so cold that he had difficulty in breathing, kicking up until he surfaced. He struck out downstream, going with the flow, swimming towards the opposite bank, hiding amongst the rocks. Grabbing hold of one he shook the water out of his eyes and looked back.

The Indians were at the creek's edge, peering into the water, looking across at the bank. Some ran along the side, stopping every now and then to try and spot him.

Asa had thought to climb out of the creek, now he didn't dare. He would be seen. And as his horse was long gone the Apaches would have no difficulty in catching him up. The safest place was to stay in the water and work his way downstream. If only it wasn't so cold.

Taking a deep breath, he went under the water again and swam as carefully as he could, trying not to make any ripples, until he had to come up for air. The

Indians were still there but not so close now. It seemed as if they were getting bored, ready to give up.

And why shouldn't they? They knew he was alone, with no horse, miles from anywhere. He couldn't go past them and get back to the stage station and it would take him a couple of days to reach Wickenburg on foot. They'd have all the time in the world to do whatever they wanted and be on their way.

The night passed slowly, each minute seeming like an hour, especially when the drumming and chanting started up again. At least, Watts thought, there wasn't the screaming of a man being tortured; but did that mean that Harrington was dead or had got away? It was terrible not knowing what was happening.

As soon as it was dawn the Indians made a quick skirmish towards the house, firing arrows, shooting, yelling.

'Just to make sure we're awake,' Watts

said grumpily, running a hand through his hair.

'How's Benny?' Sweeney demanded, coming into the bedroom.

Rose was wiping the young man's face. 'About the same. No worse anyway.'

'We've gotta get out of this place,' Sweeney said, pacing up and down. 'Those damn Indians!'

Rose wasn't quite brave enough to point out that if he hadn't sold the Indians guns they wouldn't be here now shooting at them.

'Go and get us some coffee. You go with her, kid.' Once they were gone, Sweeney bent over his brother's body. 'Benny, can you hear me?'

Benny groaned something in reply.

'We'll get out of here soon, I promise you that. I don't care what happens to anyone else but I'll take care of you.'

Rose and Timmy made coffee and took it into the parlour where everyone had gathered. They all looked exhausted, dark rings under their eyes, and dirty too. Another long, hot day stretched in front of them, with nerves on a taut wire.

'Wonder if the soldier boy got away?' Kendall said, sipping coffee as he stood at the window, peering out.

'You'd better hope so,' Mr Turner said.

'Hey!' Kendall exclaimed, standing up straight.

'What's the matter?' Watts asked.

'The Indians are up to goddamn something!'

TWENTY-ONE

Harrington opened his eyes, wondering for a moment where he was. The sun was shining in his face, that was what had woken him up, but otherwise he felt cold, which was no wonder because his clothes were wet and for some reason he was lying on his back on a pebbly beach. Suddenly remembering he sat up quickly.

He had stayed in the creek for a long time the night before, swimming underwater, coming up for air when he had to, until he'd left the Apaches far behind. When finally their cries had faded away into the distance and even the most persistent had given up trying to find him, he'd pulled himself out of the water and collapsed on to the ground. He hadn't intended to fall asleep but, exhausted, he must have done so.

And now it was morning.

Harrington stood up, stretching. It was still early, the sun was low in the sky, but it was already warm, which would help to dry his clothes.

That was about the only thing he had to be grateful for. He had left because he'd thought it the best thing to do but it had all gone wrong.

He was on his own, his horse had long gone and he had no idea of where he was; except that it was going to be a long walk to Wickenburg. In fact, after some thought he decided it would be better to forget about going there and instead return to the stage station. The Apaches wouldn't be expecting that and with luck he could slip by them.

First though he had to get to the top of the slope leading up from the creek. He stared at it. It was steep but not all that high. It shouldn't be too difficult.

He began to climb. He had to use both hands and feet to get a good grip on the rocks and once he thought he was going to fall all the way back down. He clung on, heart beating wildly, before starting up again.

He was almost at the top when he heard a noise above him. Someone coughed and then several pebbles cascaded down the slope by his head.

The Indians! They were here after all. He hadn't fooled them. They'd followed him.

But perhaps they hadn't seen him yet. Surely if they had they'd be shooting at him. Maybe he could wait, clutching at the side of the slope, hiding until they'd gone.

With sinking heart he realized that was impossible. For a hand came snaking down, grabbing his arm, pulling at him.

They'd caught him.

'What's happening?' Watts asked as he,

Sweeney and Mr Turner joined Kendall at the window.

'There.' The man pointed.

At some time during the night or perhaps early this morning the Apaches had manoeuvred the buckboard containing the furs into position a few yards away from the door. Several Indians were gathered round it.

'What are they doing?' Watts said, half to himself. Then he straightened up as he realized only too well the Indians' intention. 'Oh my God.'

'What's wrong?' Sweeney demanded.

'They're going to hide behind the buckboard, so we won't have anything to shoot at, and use it to crash against the door!'

'They won't be able to break it down, will they?' Sweeney looked at the door, which was stout and solidly barred.

'They will eventually.'

'What are we going to do?' Rose asked, hugging Timmy to her side.

'One thing is for sure, we're on our own,' Mr Turner said. 'Even if the lieutenant got away,'—his tone made that sound unlikely—'he'll never get back here with help in time.'

'He sure knew what he was doing,' Sweeney sneered.

No one took any notice. They knew Harrington had gone for the best of reasons, not because he wanted to get away, but they were too concerned with their own safety to argue with the gunrunner.

Watts took charge. 'Timmy, go back in the bedroom with Benny. Shut the door. Try to drag some furniture in front of it. Rosie, you and Mr Turner go in the kitchen.'

'Wouldn't it be better if they stayed in here?' Sweeney said. 'That's where the attack is going to be.'

'I don't suppose they'll attack from one place. That ain't all the Indians out there. Go on, Rose, now.' Once the girl had gone he turned to Sweeney. 'Look, I don't care what happens to you, your brother or your friend there. I don't particularly care what happens to me or Mr Turner.'

'But you do care about your daughter?'

'And the boy. I'm going to save two bullets, one for each of them, but I want you to promise me that if anything happens to me, then one of you will shoot them both before the Indians can get to them. You owe me that much.'

'All right.' Sweeney gave a quick nod.

'You might think about doing the same for your brother. I doubt they'll consider putting him out of his misery.'

'Let's hope it doesn't come to that.' Sweeney knew there was no way at all that he could ever shoot Benny, even if it was for Benny's own good. And he doubted whether Kendall would do so; more likely his partner would want to see Benny end up tortured by the Apaches.

'Here they come!' Kendall suddenly shouted.

Rose stood by the kitchen window, gun in her hand. She was ashamed to find she was trembling. She glanced at Mr Turner who winked at her and she tried to smile back. She wished Asa was here. Not that she believed he could work miracles but his presence was reassuring, so that it seemed while he was around nothing really bad could happen. But she knew it could. The Indians were going to make an all-out attack. Black Feather had offered them the chance of escape, a chance they'd refused. There would be no mercy.

'There's some of the bastards creeping up on us,' Mr Turner said, pointing.

Rose strained to see. She caught a glimpse of a brown body amongst clumps of scrubby grass. How many were there? She raised her gun.

Mr Turner said, 'Not yet. Not until they attack and not until you've got a clear target. Make every shot count.'

'Hey, boy, what you doing?' Benny opened

his eyes as he heard Timmy drag the chair over to the door. It was the only piece of furniture the boy could move by himself.

'The Indians are getting ready to attack. Mr Watts thought we'd be safe in here.'

'Safe?' If he'd been stronger Benny's voice would have come out as a screech, as it was it was no more than a strangled squeak. He raised himself up on his elbows, fear in his eyes. 'We won't be safe anywhere. We'll be killed for sure. Where's Leroy? I want Leroy. I don't wanna die.'

'My parents died,' Timmy said quietly. 'And it was all your fault.'

'Aw, kid, don't be like that. I didn't mean no one no harm. It wasn't my idea. It was Leroy's. I'd never have gone along with it if I'd known what would happen. I'm sorry. Say you'll protect me, won't you? You've got to. You do and I'll see you all right with Leroy, otherwise he might hurt you.'

'Once the Indians get in it won't be up to Leroy, or you, what happens. The

Indians will kill us all.'

Benny groaned. He began to wish he was still back in Yuma.

Watts, Sweeney and Kendall watched helplessly as quietly, efficiently, the Indians got behind the buckboard and started to push it towards the house. Black Feather stood a little way off, out of rifle range, surveying the scene.

'It's his plan,' Kendall said. 'I'm sure the bastard has got a smile on his face.'

'Seems fitting that you did so much hurt for them furs and now they're going to be used to kill you.'

'Shut it, old man.'

The buckboard gained momentum. It slammed into the door and the door shuddered on its hinges. The bar held this time but Watts thought it wouldn't next time.

'Get behind the table, that'll give us some protection.' He hurried over to it and pushed it on to its side, shoving the benches out of the way. As Sweeney and Kendall joined him, the buckboard smashed into the door again. 'Get ready! Here they come!'

In the kitchen Rose gave a cry as three or four lithe bodies made a dash towards the house. She and Mr Turner fired once before the Indians fell to the ground. They hadn't hit any of them.

'Oh where's Asa?' she thought.

The bar broke in two and the door gave way, falling in, crashing to the floor with a great noise and a cloud of dust.

Watts cried out. And over the pounding of his heart heard firing from the rear. This was it!

Harrington wondered what it would be like to be tortured to death. He just hoped he would die bravely but he had a feeling he'd scream and beg the last few minutes of his life away.

'Rose,' he said out loud, as strong arms dragged him over the top of the slope.

'Who?' a voice asked.

'Huh?' Harrington said in surprise and he lifted his eyes to find himself staring into the face of Fred Ulsen.

TWENTY-TWO

Behind Ulsen, Harrington saw Sergeant Johnson and the rest of the troop. They'd all gathered round to watch and he was rather surprised to find that Johnson, like Ulsen, looked pleased to see him.

'What are you doing here? How did you find me?'

'I'm a tracker, ain't I?' Ulsen said, pretending indignation. 'Are you all right? We were worried about you. You look as if you've had a run in with the Indians.'

'Yes, I have.' Harrington stood up, brushing himself down.

'You've been shot.'

'It's not bad. It doesn't hurt.' Actually it did, but Harrington was too preoccupied to worry about that right then. 'I know where the Indians are.'

'Where?'

'Watts' Stage Station.'

'That ain't too many miles away.'

'I know. I was on my way into Wickenburg to fetch help.'

'You're going the wrong way,' Johnson put in.

'I wasn't when I set out.'

'What's been happening here, Asa?'

'It's a long story, Fred. And there's no time for me to tell it at the moment. We've got to get to Watts and quick. Black Feather knows I've gone and he'll attack it as soon as it's light.'

Ulsen looked up at the sky. 'Then the attack could already have begun.'

'And I'm afraid the people there won't be able to hold out. Sergeant.' Harrington stepped forward. 'Get the men mounted and be quick about it.'

'Yes, sir.' Johnson snapped to attention as if he recognized some authority and knowledge in the lieutenant that hadn't been there before.

'And, Sergeant, have you got a horse I can use?'

'No, sir, but I'll soon find you one. Browning,' Johnson's voice rose to a shout as he strode over to the men. 'You'll ride double with Jennings. The lieutenant needs your horse.'

Before the dust had settled, several Apaches raced into the room. Watts, Sweeney and Kendall all fired and two of the Indians went down. The third was Red Lance who veered to one side and ran across the room, bullets following him but not hitting him, to the parlour door. The Indian got through it, slamming it shut behind him. Watts wanted to follow him—his daughter was back there!—but he couldn't. More Indians had already poured into the room and he and the other two were trapped by their bullets and arrows.

Suddenly Kendall gave a cry and reeled backwards with an arrow in his shoulder. He fell to the floor, screaming with pain.

'Shut up,' Sweeney snarled at him unsympathetically. He went to fire his gun; nothing happened. 'Shit, I'm outa bullets. Here, give me your gun,' and he grabbed at Kendall's revolver, turning back to shoot over the top of the table.

Watts had the satisfaction of seeing another Apache fall but with Kendall moaning and writhing in pain, there was only him and Sweeney now. They would soon be overrun.

Even as he had the thought, several of the Indians rushed at the two men, screaming their warcries as they did so.

After another sortie at the rear the Indians there didn't attack again. In fact they seemed to have disappeared.

'Where have they gone?' Rose asked, staring out of the window.

'I reckon they know the others have got in at the front and they've gone there. Your pa might need help. I'll go and see. You wait here, Rosie.'

Mr Turner went over to the door. He opened it and saw Red Lance, approaching down the hall, silent and stealthy in his moccasins. For a moment the two men looked at one another. But the younger reacted much faster than the older. Red Lance raised the pistol he held, pulled the trigger and shot Mr Turner. The man skittered back, falling heavily on the floor by Rose's feet. Blood spurted out from his chest.

'Mr Turner!' Rose cried and knelt down by the guard. She glanced up.

Red Lance stood there looking back at her. Rose's hand went to her mouth. And the Indian pulled the trigger again. This time the gun misfired. Nothing happened. Red Lance threw the gun down in disgust and reached behind him for his knife.

Somehow Rose had dropped her gun, although she couldn't remember how or why. It lay on the floor just beyond her reach. She scrambled over to pick it up. With hands that shook she hefted it up and pointed it at the young Indian who was already coming for her. He must have seen in her eyes that she would use it because he came to a halt and dived backwards even as she fired. The bullet chipped a piece out of the wall but otherwise did no harm.

Her heart beating wildly, Rose watched the hall for what seemed like a very long time but saw no more sign of the Indian.

'Oh God,' she breathed. Wiping the sweat away from her forehead she turned her attention to Mr Turner. The man didn't seem to be breathing and she knew her first task was to try and stop the bleeding. Thankful she was still wearing a skirt and not her pants, she tore off a piece of the petticoat underneath. She raised him slightly and tied it around his chest. She could do nothing more for him.

Holding the gun in both hands, the girl crouched on the floor beside the man, staring at the door until her eyes ached. What was happening? She wished she knew.

Red Lance was sure the girl with the gun wouldn't follow him but would stay with her wounded companion. They could both wait until later. He tried the door nearest to him. It wouldn't open. But it wasn't locked, something was jammed against it. It meant someone was inside. Grunting with the effort, he pushed against the door and gradually it opened wide enough for him to slip inside. He held the knife in front of him, ready for anything. Then grinned as he saw a young boy huddled over by the window and a man lying wounded in the bed.

The man started screaming. 'Shoot him, kid. Shoot him. Leroy! Help, Leroy!'

And Red Lance suddenly recognized him as one of the white men who had cheated them, sold them useless guns. And now here he was lying helpless and alone, for it was obvious that for some reason the boy wasn't about to help him, although he had a gun and could have done so. Red Lance offered up a prayer of thanks.

'Kid, shoot him! Please!' Benny yelled, as the Indian raised his knife and advanced towards the bed.

Timmy shook his head. This man and his brother were the ones responsible for his parents' deaths. And the deaths of other innocent people who'd never done the Apaches any harm but had just happened to be in the way. He didn't care what happened to Benny. He deserved killing. Timmy turned away, not wanting to see what Red Lance did.

'Kid! Kid!' Benny's voice was raised ever higher in panic.

There was another cry from Red Lance, one of triumph, followed by a gurgling sound. Followed by silence.

Timmy risked a glance round. Benny lay back in the bed, arms outstretched, a gaping wound in his chest. Red Lance was bent over him, taking his scalp. Feeling sick, Timmy quickly looked away again. Red Lance cried out and Timmy stiffened sure he was going to be killed as well. Nothing happened. And the next time he looked round he saw the room was empty, except for the dead man in the bed.

Timmy felt neither sorrow nor satisfaction. He felt only numb.

At the head of the troop, Harrington came to a halt about half a mile from the stage station. Even from this far away the sound of firing could be heard while smoke drifted up from the house. They couldn't be too late, he thought, they mustn't be. Was Rose all right? Please, let her be. If anything had happened to them he'd never forgive himself for leaving them alone.

'Sergeant, get the bugler to blow the charge. As loud as he can. The rest of you make as much noise as possible. Warn the Indians we're here and send hope to the besieged.'

'Yes, sir.'

The bugler came to the front of the soldiers and blew the signal for an all-out charge.

Harrington raised his arm. 'Good luck everyone. All right, troop, let's go!'

He dug spurs into his horse's sides and sent it galloping forward. He prayed that they would get there in time.

TWENTY-THREE

The young Indian flung himself at Watts. Watts managed to bring his gun up, knocking his attacker on the side of the head so that he staggered away. The respite was short. Another Indian immediately took his place. Beside him, Sweeney went down on the floor overpowered by two Apaches. Watts was knocked off his feet. The end couldn't be far away now.

From outside, still a long way away—but not so far it couldn't easily be heard—came the sound of a bugle.

An army bugler blowing the charge!

Help had arrived!

Sweeney stuck his gun in the stomach of one of the Apaches attacking him and pulled the trigger even as the second one jumped up. At the same time Red Lance appeared in the doorway. He was yelling and signalling.

The pounding of horses' hooves, shouting, came on the air to the besieged.

Red Lance led the retreat out of the house.

Slowly Watts got up. He was trembling violently and hastily he holstered his gun, scared he might fire it by mistake. He looked round his home. Three or four dead Apaches lay near the door, the wounded had been dragged away. Sweeney seemed unhurt, except for several bruises on his face, and Kendall although in pain, was still alive.

Watts didn't care about either of them and he shoved Sweeney aside. 'Rose! Timmy!' He was met in the doorway by his daughter.

'Pa,' she said hesitantly.

Watts took her in his arms and she burst out crying.

'Have they really gone?'

'Yeah. The army is here.'

'Is it Asa?'

'I don't know.'

Oh please let it be, Rose thought, please let him be here, let him be safe and well.

As Harrington and the troop neared the stage station, they saw the Apaches stream from the building and start to make their escape in all directions.

'Sergeant Johnson, Fred, go after them!' he ordered. 'Round up as many of them as you can.'

'What about you?' Ulsen asked.

'I'm going to see how the folks in the house are.' Harrington didn't stop to see Johnson divide the troop so the men could take after the fleeing Indians, he urged his horse on, wondering what he was going to find.

Sweeney hauled Kendall to his feet. 'Come on, let's get the hell outa here before the goddamned army arrives.'

Kendall moaned, clutching at his shoulder.

'Can you ride?'

'I'll manage.' Kendall was hurt, in pain, but no way was he going to let Sweeney leave him behind so that he could take all the blame and all the punishment. 'What about the furs?'

'Damn the furs. We ain't got time to worry about them. Let's get my brother and go!'

'Let's take the girl too.'

Sweeney's eyes flickered. 'Yeah, OK, maybe a hostage would be useful.'

'It ain't a hostage I'm thinking of.'

'Let's just go.' Supporting Kendall, Sweeney pushed by Watts and Rose and into the bedroom. 'Oh no! Oh Christ! Oh no!'

Kendall, Watts and Rose crowded in the doorway behind him. Benny lay in the bed, obviously dead, while Timmy crouched on the floor. Rose swallowed hard, she'd never seen anyone scalped before. Watts kept a firm arm around her, supporting her.

'Benny! Benny!' Sweeney said, going over to his brother and shaking him. 'Benny, wake up. We've got to go. Cliff, help me.'

'For Chrissakes, Leroy, he's dead! Forget him. He weren't no use anyway. Come on, girl, you're coming with us.'

'No you don't!' Watts said, pushing Rose behind him. 'You leave her be.' He went for his gun but before he could pull it out of its holster, Sweeney had drawn his revolver. Watts was sure the man was going to kill them all as a punishment for Benny's death.

But saying, 'You bastard you never did like Benny!' he shot Kendall in the throat.

Rose cried out in alarm as the man collapsed back against the wall, slowly sliding down it, leaving a gash of blood behind him. 'Timmy, come here, quick!'

As the boy jumped up, Sweeney grabbed hold of his arm. 'No you don't. You were meant to protect Benny. You let him die. You come along.'

'Don't be stupid, Sweeney, he couldn't do anything. He's just a boy.'

'Stop it.' Rose dashed forward.

But Sweeney was beyond reasoning and he shoved her aside so viciously she fell over. He pointed his gun at Watts, looking wild eyed enough to shoot anyone who got in his way. Hauling a frightened Timmy after him, he hurried through to the back of the house, kicked Mr Turner aside, and went out into the yard. He looked round frantically. A horse, he needed a horse.

At the same time Harrington arrived at the front. Seeing the buckboard and the broken-down door, he flung himself off his horse and ran into the stage station; almost falling over the bodies, taking in the mess of a room—the overturned table, broken crockery—that had once been so neat and tidy. Christ, he was too late, he knew he was.

'Rose! Mr Watts! Rose!'

'Here,' Watts yelled in reply. 'We're safe.'

Asa gulped down several sighs of relief as Rose came running towards him. He caught her up in his arms, hugging her close, never wanting to let her go. 'Oh, Rose, I was so worried about you.'

'I thought you were dead.'

'I got away. Are you really all right?'

'Yes. Really. But, Asa,' Rose said, and pulled away from him, 'Sweeney's got Tim.'

'What!'

'Sweeney blames him for Benny's death. He'll kill him. You must go after him.'

'I can't leave you.'

'You must. For Tim. Go on, please.' She gave him a little push. 'I'll be waiting for you.'

And however reluctant Harrington was to leave Rose now that he had found her again he knew he couldn't let Timmy be taken away by Leroy Sweeney. Giving the girl a kiss on the cheek he went out to his horse, leaping into the saddle. He rode round to the back of the house.

There, not too far away, he saw Sweeney and Timmy. They were sharing an Indian paint pony.

Harrington set off in pursuit.

TWENTY-FOUR

Realizing he was being chased, Sweeney urged the pony on faster. Now and then he glanced over his shoulder to see where his pursuer was but he didn't waste time turning to shoot at him. Harrington didn't fire either. He didn't want to risk hitting Timmy.

They galloped across the dusty plain towards the foothills beyond the creek. Harrington's horse was tired but the paint pony was carrying two and gradually he gained on them.

Sweeney came to the hills and not wanting to lose him, Harrington urged his horse into one last bigger effort. Some boulders loomed up ahead and he rounded them. Beyond was a high slope, dotted with mesquite bushes and more rocks. Halfway up Sweeney had come to a halt. Suspecting some sort of ambush, Harrington immediately drew his own sweating stumbling animal to a stop. Then he saw that it wasn't an ambush at all. At least not one set by Sweeney.

At the top of the slope two Indians sat on horses, waiting and watching. He recognized Black Feather and Red Lance.

Sweeney looked both up and down the slope, seeking escape. Suddenly Timmy slid off the horse. Sweeney made a grab for him but missed and the boy ran for the safety of some boulders. Leroy was on his own—no hostage, just one gun—between two sets of enemies.

Harrington kicked his horse into a walk. He pretended to himself that he hoped Sweeney would give up so he could take him back to stand trial, but deep down he knew he hoped Sweeney would do no such thing.

Sweeney didn't. He had no intention of being taken anywhere just to finish up at the end of a hangman's noose. He stared at the Indians. They hadn't moved, made no threat against him, but it was obvious he'd never get by them. Harrington, the soldier boy, was the better bet. He drew his gun and, yelling, charged at Asa.

Harrington didn't hesitate. Calmly he halted the horse and pulled out his own revolver. Holding it with both hands he aimed carefully. He took no notice of the bullets from Sweeney's gun. Instead he fired, three times, so fast that, although Sweeney was tumbling backwards from the first shot, all three bullets struck him in the chest. Sweeney landed on the ground, bounced and rolled, and came to a halt.

Harrington looked up at the two Indians. His gun was empty and he wouldn't have time to reload if they decided to attack. Instead they stared back at him for a few moments then simply rode away, disappearing over the brow of the hill.

'Lieutenant! Lieutenant!' Timmy's cry came to Harrington as he bent forward over his saddlehorn, breathing deeply. The boy emerged from his hiding place and ran down the hill towards him.

'What's happening, Sergeant?' Harrington asked as they got back to the stage station.

'Sir,' Johnson saluted smartly. 'We caught a couple of the Apaches who were wounded but the rest got away.'

'They won't cause any more trouble,' Ulsen put in, reaching up to help Timmy from the horse. 'I reckon by the time we get to Fort Fenton we'll find that the Apaches are all back on the Reservation, sorry for their sins and themselves, and receiving hand-outs again. I don't suppose anyone will make any charges against them.'

'You're probably right,' Harrington agreed. 'Especially now the bastards who sold them the guns in the first place are all dead. Sergeant, I want you to detail some men to help these folks here. There are people to bury, rooms to tidy up. And we'll take the gunrunners back to the fort to be buried. The Watts won't want any reminder of them.'

'Asa,' Ulsen said, with a twinkle in his eyes, 'looks to me like you've got unfinished business of your own here.'

And Harrington looked over his shoulder to see Rose Watts standing in the doorway of her home, watching him anxiously. He smiled. 'Tim, go to Rose. Tell her I'll be there as soon as I can.'

It was late evening before the troop was ready to start back for Fort Fenton. Timmy wasn't going with them. He'd been offered a home with Rose and her father.

'You'll like that won't you?' Harrington said, ruffling his hair.

'Yes, sir. Very much. Although I'll miss you,' Timmy added shyly.

'I'll miss you too but I'll be by to see you soon.'

'He's a good boy,' Rose said, watching as he went to join Watts in seeing to the horses. 'He'll be happy enough here helping Pa. Perhaps in time he'll forget all that happened.' She turned back to Asa. 'I wish you weren't going.'

'I wish I didn't have to. But I have to do my duty.' He smiled. 'But Fort Fenton isn't so very far away, is it?'

'You meant what you said? You will come back to see us?'

'Try keeping me away. I'm quite sure I can lead several patrols this way in the not too distant future. I love you, Rose, you know that don't you?'

'Yes.'

'You'll make a good lieutenant's wife.'

'After what you've done here if you're not made captain I shall want to know the reason why.'

And not caring that everyone was watching them, Harrington took Rose in his arms and kissed her.

Rose, Timmy, Watts and a bandaged-up Mr Turner all stood watching and waving as Harrington led the troop away. He turned in his saddle several times to wave back, much to the amusement of his men. He didn't care, he wasn't lonely any more. He had Rose, he had Timmy. They were the ones he cared about, the ones who cared for him. A family of his own.

The last time he looked a stagecoach rumbled over the distant horizon, approaching Watts' Stage Station.

Everything was back to normal.